UNICORNS, FEY, & A HARDBOILED DAME

UNICORNS, FEY, & A HARDBOILED DAME

THE MIRIAM ASTER DUOLOGY

PETER M. BALL

Eclectic Projects (an imprint of Brain Jar Press)
PO Box 6687
Upper Mt Gravatt, QLD, 4122
Australia
Eclectic Projects: www.PeterMBall.com
Brain Jar Press: www.BrainJarPress.com

Cover design by Brain Jar Press
Cover Images : *Unicorn Silhouette* © Arak Rattanawijittakorn/Shutterstock, *Grunge Border* © Gordan/Shutterstock © *Paper Texture*, nekotaro/Shutterstock

ISBN: 978-1-922479-44-0 (Ebook) | 978-1-922479-45-7 (Paperback)

CONTENTS

HORN

CHAPTER 1

The phone call came at three am, about a half-hour after the body arrived at the morgue. It didn't wake me. I don't sleep well, not anymore. I used to work Homicide back when my life made sense and insomnia's one of those bad habits I picked up on the job, right up there with the cigarettes and the tendency towards one glass of gin too many. It's just another little twitch to remind me that my body doesn't pay attention to the lies I tell myself about the past.

My name's Miriam Aster. Ask most of the cops I used to work with and they'll tell you that now I'm a freelance detective, an ice-hearted bitch, or a fucked-up lush who killed her own career. Pick one, they're all right. I was busy feeling sorry for myself when the call came through. The phone went to voicemail and I ignored the insistent beep that told me they'd left a message. They rang back. Twice.

I watched my phone vibrate along with the ringtone, rattling across the bedside table. It should've been a relief to hear it – a three am call meant a desperate client, and I knew the kind of money the desperate threw around. I spent two minutes pretending I didn't care about paying rent before I rewarded their persistence and flipped the receiver open.

"Aster?" It was a man's voice, surly and brusque; familiar enough for me to figure it for Tim Kesey. A bad feeling twisted into my stomach and stuck there like a fishhook. Kesey hasn't exactly approved of me since I was booted off the Force. He hadn't actually liked me since I slept with his sister, but you know the old saying: some mistakes you regret, some mistakes you celebrate.

"Tim?" My voice snarled, anger seeping through.

"Aster, we need you." Kesey sounded older, a little more worn around the edges and wary about talking to me. I double-checked the caller ID to be sure it was him. "Listen Aster, I know it's late, but Heath's insisting. We need to bring you in, off the books, as a consultant. You up for it?"

I groped for the rumpled soft pack of Camels by my bed, then realised my lighter had fallen off the bedside table. I sighed, letting the weariness creep into my voice. "It's still early by my watch. Intrigue me."

"We've got a body. A kid." I could hear the buzz of a crowd filtering in from his side of the call, the momentary chirp of a police siren as a car pulled in. "Heath says we need you on it. Wake the fuck up."

"I'm awake," I said, and I was. The old instincts still triggered when someone mentioned a body, even if it'd been a decade since corpses were a part of my daily business. "How old's the kid?"

"Ask Heath when you see him. If you're on the job." My searching fingers found a glass instead of the lighter. There was a shallow mouthful of gin settled in the base. I took the cigarette out of my mouth and drank instead, a precaution against the way Kesey's tone was setting my teeth on edge. He was the kind of cop who was big on protocol but it wasn't like him to be evasive. Half the reason he avoided calling me in was his dislike of ambiguity on his paperwork — the Department tended to list me as a consulting specialist and leave the details blank when they filled in the books.

"Sure, I'm on the job," I said, "if you're willing to pay the consulting fee. I don't work cheap anymore. Not even for old friends." Then I named an hourly rate, a big one. I expected Kesey to swear at me, fuck off, and let me get to sleep, but he didn't. "Fine," he said. "Come in on this, play it by the book for once, and log your time with the precinct. I'll pay you any fee you want, Aster. Just get to the morgue. Fast. Got it?"

"You're getting soft, Tim."

"Don't give me shit unless you're here, doing the job. The money doesn't matter, not this time."

I figured that for bullshit. I'm not the kind of girl who believes anyone when they say that, least of all a bastard like Kesey. "The money always matters," I said. "Tell Heath I'm on my way."

I hung up and considered the bottle sitting on my bedside table. Decided against it and pulled on one of my better suits, a charcoal pin-stripe over a black turtleneck instead of a button-down shirt. It's my meeting money outfit. The one I break out to give an illusion of respectability around clients who were nervous about airing their dirty laundry with a stranger. Not the kind of look you needed when consulting on a murder case, but I figured what the hell - if Kesey's got money to throw around, I might as well look the part while putting my two cents in.

The early hours of the morning are a bad time to hit the city morgue, but I tend to hate it more than most. If you dig beneath the t-shirts and turtlenecks that make up my wardrobe there's a big Y-shaped scar running down my chest, the two arms starting beneath my collar bone, meeting the downward cut between my breasts. It's a big, ugly thing, thick and purple; a lingering reminder of my first-hand experience with the autopsy slab. Don't get too curious, there's not much of a story behind it; once upon a time I fell in love and got involved in some trouble on her behalf. When I ended up dead she pulled some strings and got me back. It seems like a good deal on the surface, but you don't bounce back from something like that. My life turned to shit afterwards and my heart got broke. The rest just isn't worth talking about.

I sat out the front for a bit, putting it all off with another cigarette, watching the glum square of light spilling out of an office window on the top floor. The morgue and I have had plenty of chances to get reacquainted under better circumstances, but it hasn't done much to help my nerves. Something bad was going down inside. I could feel that familiar itch on the back of my neck, the same one I always got when the weird shit started. I smoked, hoping the itch would go away, and wished I'd asked Kesey for more money.

I was looking for Heath Morrow, a morgue institution. Heath was bottom of the whole freaky pile when it came to the city coroners. He preferred working the late shift and had a fetish for the odd cases, which meant he called me in every chance he got. I should have hated Heath, but we got on okay. For all his ambient creepiness, he never assumed I was crazy and he'd become a lot more bearable since I'd come back to life on his autopsy table. His tendency to talk to my chest vanished after he'd cut me open. Apparently it's hard to objectify someone once you've had a scalpel poking around their innards.

I found him sitting in front of his computer, hunched over the keyboard like a wire-thin mannequin with too-long arms. He was transcribing autopsy notes in one window, fingers hammering the keys as he listened to the mp3 recording of his own voice explaining his actions. Another open window streamed grainy, greyscale porn from one of those poorly dubbed Russian sex sites, filling the computer speakers with tinny moans and the wet slap of flesh on flesh. One of the black-and-white nudes started groaning, heading for climax, and a second figure turned to smile at the camera. He had ridiculous fangs, probably fake. They hung down from his gums like cigarettes, but the blood trailing down the nude girl's neck looked real enough for video; black ink on white flesh, it did the job. I rolled my eyes and coughed, just loud enough to warn Heath I was there. He bounced, startled. "So," I said. "How's things?"

He spun on his office chair, all smiles and crazy hair. "About fucking time," Heath said. "We got a live one for you." In Heath's world this passed as a joke, but I was too tired to offer a courtesy laugh. I gave him a beat to realise the comment had flopped, then asked the question of the hour: "Where's Kesey?"

"Back at the crime scene." Heath switched off the porn and

his smile stretched out a little, showing off the bad teeth. "You know how he gets. Things are a little too weird here for his taste, plus, you know—" He nodded at me and spread his hands. "I kinda had to push to get you signed on to this one, Aster."

He tossed a thin folder on the bench, started twisting in his office chair as I picked the paperwork up and flicked through. Sally Crown, age fourteen. Reported missing a year back, found facedown in a dumpster, wearing baby doll makeup and a plastic tiara, a little under an hour ago. Nothing in the file made it worth paying the kind of money I was asking. I looked up over the edge of the folder, flicking through the crime scene photos without really looking.

"You want to summarise, Heath?"

He shrugged. "External bruising suggests she's been the victim of blunt trauma to the back of the head and shoulders, the kind of impact you'd get if you were dropped. No broken bones, so I'm assuming it was a short fall. If it was a fall. There's some doubt there. It doesn't quite add up. She's got some fresher lesions on her scalp and neck, consistent with being dragged by the feet or scraped along the ground, probably posthumously."

"And I'm here because?" Heath's grin threatened to slit his face open.

"Mystery details," he said. "I didn't want to write them up until you had a chance to look at them, just in case and all that. Follow me." He led me down the dark corridors into the bowels of the morgue, stepping into one of the sealed autopsy rooms that they used for infectious work. Heath hadn't bothered to put the warning light on but I worried just the same. The room was a frozen box that stank of formaldehyde and stale blood. Sally Crown was laid out on the table, street-kid thin and pale even before she'd become a corpse. Heath had her opened up already, ribs folded back like origami wings. My chest twinged in sympathy, my scars itchy. "Meet Sally," Heath said. "She's our little conundrum for the evening. Take a look."

I snapped on the latex and looked. I'm no expert, but I've watched enough autopsies in real time to know the basics. Her abdomen was distended and firm to touch, her upper thighs and lower stomach marked with thin red lines. It wasn't a good sign. I glanced over at Heath. "You find any trace evidence?"

Heath grabbed a clipboard, paging through his notes. "Powder beneath the fingernails, probably makeup. Some white fibres caught in the toenail, probably fur. Lots of body glitter, all over. Not just the face. We're still waiting on the lab reports, but they take time. You know how it is."

I grunted and the suspicion in my gut started to spread, flowering into real fear. I patted down my pockets until I found my cigarettes. I tapped one out and flipped it into my mouth. Heath started to say something, then thought better of it. "Let me guess," I said, lighting up. "There's evidence of bruising and internal bleeding in the vaginal cavity, injuries consistent with rape victims assaulted by a sharp object?"

Heath nodded, grinning. He was enjoying this a little too much. "It gets weirder."

"I'll bet." I closed my eyes and went with my gut. "Scars on the hymen, like it'd healed up after it had been ripped. Glitter in the vaginal cavity? Glowing maggots in the uterus?"

Heath's smile vanished. "Yeah," he said. "How'd you know?"

"I've seen this before," I said. Heath grabbed a pair of forceps and folded back the cut along the uterus. You could see the formless shapes within, tumbling and wiggling in the fleshy sack of the womb. The largest of them was already glowing, its sulphurous light disguising tiny arms and legs as they grew from the pearlescent blob. Another hour and it'd be done, a wisp of malicious magic in an inherited human form. "Fuck." I breathed against the cigarette so I didn't have to smell the noxious, sugary scent that rose up. "She's been raped by a unicorn."

Heath dropped his gaze into the squirming mess, frowning. "You can tell that from maggots?"

"A unicorn in heat is basically a big dick," I said. "That's why they have the horn. Fey, unicorns, the lot of them, they procreate using belief, and it's fucking hard to avoid believing in something that's sticking twelve inches of horn inside you." Heath was still frowning at me, and I shrugged. I've been around, but I'm far from an expert. I shouldn't have been his first port of call when it came to stuff like this and we both knew it.

"You've called her?" I asked, and Heath nodded. "She have anything to say?"

He didn't need to ask who I was talking about. "She recommended calling you."

"Figures." I shook my head. "You're going to have to burn the body. Fast."

"Why?"

One of the glowing maggots started to crawl free of the mass, its tiny form shuddering as the mutation began. I swore and buried it beneath the tip of my cigarette, the smell of burning sugar mingling with the formaldehyde stink.

"Because an hour from now every one of those maggots will look like a six inch human with wings," I said. "And every single one of the fuckers is going to be hungry for blood."

CHAPTER 2

I got coffee while Heath did the disposal, punching the buttons for black with two sugars into the vending machine in the foyer. My hands shook when I lifted the paper cup, the room eerie and silent once the coffee was brewed. Part of me was back in my shitty apartment, still woozy from an evening with too much gin and too little sleep. The rest of me was pretending I hadn't just told Heath to commit another felony. Somewhere in the bowels of the building, he was feeding the corpse of Sally Crown into the morgue incinerator and hundreds of newborn fairies were dying. By the time he rejoined me I'd emptied my first coffee into the wastepaper basket, undrunk, and started feeding change into the slot so I could order a second.

"I've got a percolator in the office," he said, hovering by the door.

I shook my head. "I've drunk your coffee. It tastes like tar."

"The machine stuff's not much better."

It wasn't, but I wasn't really after coffee. The solid clink of coins nesting inside the machine soothed the jagged edge of my nerves. I could imagine the parts inside, working to a coordinated rhythm to deliver my coffee and add the sweetener. Given enough time and access to a computer I could find out how it worked on the internet, understand all the science and engineering behind it. The machine was rational, understandable, and real.

"I've got donuts, if you're hungry," Heath said.

I ignored him, busied myself with the fresh paper cup. "A unicorn." The scar running down my chest ached, the pain dull and insistent. "Fuck, another one."

"I called Kesey and passed along the good news. He threatened to fire me for destroying evidence in an ongoing investigation."

"Had to be done," I said, and Heath shrugged. There was a smudge of ash on the edge of his cheeks, a thin crease of black in the crevice of his nails. Stuff like this was done off the books, and Heath knew better than to leave the ashes where they could be found. "I was going to call Anya," he said. "Keep her informed, since it's her purview and all. Unless you want to do it?"

I shook my head. "I'm done with the fey. I'm working for you and Kesey," I said. "I'm an advisor, nothing more. I came, I saw, I advised."

Heath nodded. He was fresh to the job last time there was a unicorn loose in the city, a gangly kid straight out of medical school and obsessed with the dead. Good at what he did, sure, but kept in the dark more often than not. He never would have heard of Anya Titan if he hadn't been on duty the night I turned up dead. She called him while he was doing the autopsy and suggested putting me back together and stitching me up before I came to. Anya frightened him, back then. I had a sneaking suspicion that these days he had her on speed dial.

"I gotta tell you, Heath, it worries me that you keep in touch with her." He retreated into his office, and I trailed along behind. Heath busied himself with scrubbing the ash off his hands at the small sink in the corner. I angled myself to glare at his reflection. "Anya isn't safe."

"She's safe enough as long as I don't get too close, and she needed a new pair of hands after you were turfed out." He soaped up, watching my reflection in the mirror above the sink. "House of secrets and all that. Even she needs a favour done every now and then."

I shook my head to shut him up. I knew the drill, had recited it myself when I was the one keeping Anya's secrets. That's the way she worked; you kept secrets for the common good, traded favours with her because that's the way it had to be. It'd cost me my job when I got in too deep, cost me even more than that in the long run. "The favours you end up doing for her are rarely the problem."

I scratched at my chest, my smile grim. I told myself Heath was a big boy and tried to let the past go. "Fuck it, if we keep this up, I'm going to need a drink."

"Scotch in my desk drawer," Heath said. "Help yourself."

If I was smart I would have taken him up on the offer. "No, I'm working. You're a bad influence, Heath Morrow, and it's late. I'll give you a list of people to chase down who can help you find the fairy horse; pass it on to Kesey."

Heath turned, wiping long fingers on a grubby towel. Scrubbing had done little to remove the black ash under his fingernails. "You're seriously going to sit this out?"

"I seriously am. I'll send Tim the bill."

Heath scrubbed a hand through his hair, refusing to meet my eyes. "Listen, before you clock off, Kesey called – he wants to see you."

"He never wants to see me."

"This time he does." He gave me the address of the crime scene, grinning. "I guess hell froze over or something."

His good humour faded the moment I checked the details and started swearing.

They found Sally Crown in an alleyway off Carmody Street, her corpse discovered by a pair of beat cops who lucked onto it while chasing a purse snatcher. Heath's directions to the crime scene were vague, but I knew the area well enough to place it. It was a little dogleg laneway tucked behind a row of Asian restaurants and cut-price liquor stores. It smelt of rot and cardamom and cinnamon-sharp curry powder. The entire place gave me a bad feeling of déjà vu.

I showed my ID at the crowd control perimeter and walked

in, found Kesey giving orders to a pack of uniforms. "Aster," he said, nodding. He straightened up, doing his best to loom. I shuffled into his shadow and lit another cigarette. Kesey never changed, not where it counted. He just replaced the size and stiffness of the stick up his arse and put on a little bulk around the stomach every time they gave him a promotion. He glared at me. "Thanks for coming."

"Good to see you again, Tim," I said. "How's your sister?" I watched what little goodwill he had left for me drain out of his face, his mouth twisting into a stiff sneer. I gave him a bland smile, sweet and innocent.

"The morgue called," he said. "Heath was saying something about fairies."

"Unicorn," I told him. "You've got a problem with a unicorn. A big one."

Kesey leaned over me. He had a mean face, the kind that accepted years of weathered abuse and locked itself into a permanent frown as an act of self-defence. I stood my ground; Kesey was a foot taller than I was and had plenty of extra weight to throw around, but we both knew who'd win if it came down to a fight. He believed in rules and I didn't. That'd come in handy the last time he'd pushed the issue. "I hope this isn't a joke, Aster," he said. "This is a dead girl, and if I find out you're stringing this along because you need to make rent-"

I held up a hand. "You called me, Tim. I can walk, if you want. I was ready to, back at the morgue. If not, I'll give you what you paid for. You got unicorns, okay? White horse, big horn, nasty attitude. I guarantee you it's worse than you're thinking." Kesey fumed. I ignored him and looked into the alley, watching the flashlights strobe as the cops searched for clues. "Is it safe to go in, or is forensics going to jump all over me?"

Kesey lifted the tape. "Just put out the cigarette before you stomp around. The entire scene's been contaminated enough." He rolled his eyes. "Beat cops."

The smell hit me twenty feet down the alleyway, a subtle blend of hickory smoke and hothouse flowers. Anya's smell, distinctive as a fingerprint. For a moment I felt like I'd stepped back ten years; cutting through the alley after an Indian meal, our bellies full of korma and our hands beginning to wander. I'm twenty-eight again, in love and full of promise, the youngest homicide detective in city history. Three steps later I was back in the present, years settling over me with the stench of rotting vegetables and week-old naan. Kesey looked at me, scowling, his mouth open and working. I couldn't hear a damn thing he was saying. I shook the feeling off, focused on his face. "I missed that."

Kesey gazed into the gloom of the alley, his flashlight a bright sheen as it worked its way across the garbage bags and chipped backdoors. He rolled his eyes and sighed. "Bad place for a kid to die," he said. I gave him a grim smile through the gloom.

"She didn't die here." I fished a penlight out of my jacket pocket and clicked it on, joining the searchers as they scoured the grey concrete. "This is just the place they dumped her body."

Kesey's eyebrows shot up. "They?"

"They," I said. I pointed my flashlight at the dumpster. It was squat and rusting, stained with red streaks in the light blue steel. I tried to imagine Sally Crown's body inside it and shuddered. "No unicorn is dumping a body in a thing like that on its own."

"How do you know?" Kesey frowned. I held both hands up in front of his face, waggling my thumbs in tandem.

"No thumbs," I said. "It makes lifting lids hard, and the report said it was closed when the body was found."

"Could have nudged it." Kesey threw his hip against the steel, checking the weight. "Dump the body while it was open, then shove it until the lid fell."

"Doesn't wash either." I rapped the side of the dumpster, listened to the muted bong it made. "Steel. Your average exile can handle it, if they have to, but the unicorn's pure fey and they treat the shit like poison. Can't touch anything that rusts; the sensation is supposed to be kinda like pushing your hand down on a razor blade."

"Christ." Kesey killed the light on his torch and leaned up against the wall, hand running through his thinning hair. "I'm getting too old for this bullshit, Aster. It was bad enough the first time around." He said it calm, casual, but it was a baited hook and we both knew it. Kesey wasn't big on trust at the best of times, and I'd violated his a dozen times back when I carried a badge.

"You could sink the file," I said. "That's what they do, most places. Write it off, bury it as a cold case, forget it ever happened." Kesey shook his head, an angry gleam in his eyes. He was old school, in more ways than one, the kind of cop you always dream of when you make up something like "to protect and serve". The way he figured, his city wasn't going to run like most places, even if he didn't always understand what happened inside the city limits. That's the only reason he tolerated having me there, earning my fee as a special consultant by giving him the lowdown on things he didn't want to believe in. I left him to his angst and started poking around the alley. "Have you found anything else out here? Fur, glitter, bone fragments. Anything but the body?"

"It's clean."

The itch came back, the same one I always got when magic was around. I closed my eyes and breathed in, tasted a lung full of hickory smoke, felt the ghost-memory of Anya's hand working its way down the length of my spine. I gritted my teeth and ignored it. Kesey stepped towards the police line, right into a puddle of day-old curry sauce.

"Listen, Tim, I got a bad feeling about this one." He looked at me, shaking curry off his foot. "I'm not saying I won't work it, but I'm not doing it hands-on, okay? I'm here to advise, to give you what you need, and your boys handle it from there."

"Right." Kesey gave me a long look, calculating, and walked away. I followed him back to the police line, watching the puke-yellow footprints he left behind as he scraped his shoes across the bitumen. "Advise and let us do our jobs," he said. "That's the point of consulting, anyway, isn't it? Just do the fucking job, Aster. I want this shit put away - get me a lead and point me in the right direction. Then you can tell your friends that it doesn't ever fucking happen here again."

I opened my mouth, ready to tell him they weren't my

fucking friends anymore, caught the whispering press of a phantom tongue writhing against mine. I started, surprised, and Kesey was gone before I recovered. Sunlight crept up over the horizon as I climbed into my car, still feeling the faint press of Anya's kisses brushing against my lips.

CHAPTER 3

I spent about twenty minutes sitting in my car, watching the uniforms work crowd control as the early morning joggers and dog-walkers started wandering over to check out the commotion. I'll never understand people who get up before five. My eyes hurt from too little sleep and my stomach churned with an oily fusion of bad coffee, gin and hunger. I should have gone home. I don't make good decisions in the early hours of the morning and Kesey would've had my licence if he knew where I was going instead. I stalled for time, counting the number of day-glo jogging suits in the crowd. Three blue, one pink, two a sickly shade of yellow. Eventually I dug my phone out of my pocket and dialled the direct line to the morgue office.

"This is Morrow. Go."

I took a deep breath. "Heath, I need her address."

"Aster?" He sounded wary.

"She's all over the goddamn crime scene, Heath. So many memories of Anya it could have been an episode of *This is Your Life*."

"You told Kesey?"

"What do you think?" The silence on the end of the phone said everything that needed saying. My gut said putting Kesey and Anya together was a bad idea. Kesey's approach to the weird stuff had always been complicated, and Anya had a way of making expediency sound more attractive than procedure. "Kesey wants the horse gone, he doesn't care about the paper trail. I wouldn't be here otherwise, yeah?"

"Maybe. Maybe you just want to see her. It could be wishful thinking; a unicorn shows up, you see all these signs-"

I smashed a fist into my steering wheel, pain sparking down my arm. "I don't think about her, Heath." I said, my voice cold and even. "Ever. Got it?"

"Whatever you say." I could tell he was smirking. "She hasn't moved; same address as before. I'll send it over if you don't remember."

I hung up before he had a chance to become a complete idiot. I remembered how to get there well enough.

The last time I'd been to Anya's place I was three days away from losing my badge and the spectre of internal affairs hovered over me while they investigated a shooting I'd written up as self defence. It didn't go well. We'd dated for three years, me doing favours for her the entire way, but the shooting was the first time I felt like I'd crossed a line. Maybe I'm wrong about that. When you ask questions for a living, you get used to truth being fluid.

Think of it this way: most people get through their entire lives without encountering something big, something that rewrites their perceptions and tells them they're not alone in the world. We call those people lucky. Some people brush up against the strangeness and disregard it as unimportant; you see them at parties, talking about how their flat is haunted or they think they saw some strange lights while they were cruising the highway at four in the morning. Humanity, as a species, is fucking aces at denial, and you can tell those people talking about their haunted flats don't really believe what they saw. If they did they wouldn't be talking about it, bragging about it almost, like they wanted it to happen again.

Other people get touched by the strangeness, up close and personal. Usually they end up in morgues; the rest of us learn to cope. That's why I worked with her. Anya-fucking-Titan was my first brush with strangeness, as up close and personal as it gets.

She lived in the kind of building estate agents described as *full of bohemian charm*, which largely meant it was an old thirties motel that'd become dilapidated enough to rent the rooms on the cheap permanent lease. Ten years back it'd been full of junkies and heavy metal drummers, but Westbury had flourished and become the hotspot for young up-and-coming artists of all stripes. I guess it cut down on the number of drummers in the area, but there were still plenty of drugs. I climbed up the rickety stairs that linked the long halls full of revamped art deco doorframes. Anya was on the fifth floor, her door painted the same shade of candy-pale green as I remembered. I started wearing my knuckles thin on the woodwork. It was early, just coming up on five-thirty, but Anya wasn't big on sleep. It took ten minutes of hammering before she came to let me in, but she was well-dressed and perfectly coifed as she opened the door. "Aster," she said. "You look like shit."

"Late night," I told her, and we stood there for a while, watching one another and letting the silence stretch out. I drank in the details of her: the moor-wild hair, the mis-matched eyes in two different shades of violet, the sharp points of her nose and eyebrows. I felt a sting in the part of my heart that never really healed after I left her, just scabbed over while I got on with things and tried not to pick at the wound. "It's business," I said. "And, to be honest, I'm too tired to fuck around with this. Let me in and give me coffee."

Anya shrugged and stood aside. Her apartment was gaudy, but comfortable enough once you got used to the clashing colours. Antique furniture, vases filled with snapdragons and daisies, her coffee table overflowing with books and shiny baubles. Anya disappeared into the small kitchenette. I could hear water running as she filled up the jug. Everything smelt of her; hickory smoke and perfume.

"A unicorn killed a fourteen year old girl this morning," I said. I didn't get an answer. "Her name was Sally Crown, a runaway. Turns out it was in heat. There were spawn in her womb, but we got to them in time." I looked up and Anya was standing at the doorway, watching me with her mismatched eyes.

"What's that got to do with me?"

I quirked an eyebrow. "You're kidding, right?"

She blinked and her eyes changed colour, the violet turning turquoise in the dim light. "This sounds like you're on a case, Aster. You weren't doing that anymore. No more chasing the fey, no more coming around here looking for favours, no more compromising the truth to keep people safe. Isn't that what you told me?"

"Things change."

"Yes," Anya said. "They do. You stopped investigating murders and I stopped working as the gatekeeper when they closed the gate. I'm barely involved in anything these days, and I'm exiled now, remember? There are limits to what I can do, and we aren't going back to the good old days."

I snorted and reached over the coffee table, flipped one of her books so I could look at the photo on the back cover. Anya in a white suit and scarf, looking away from the camera and smiling. She hadn't aged since I left her. "It's a unicorn," I said. "They gave the case to Kesey, and he knows just enough to know he hasn't got a clue how to stop the damn thing, which means it comes down to me. They need someone to handle the weird shit and I got lumped with the job."

Anya stared at me. She didn't blink. I stamped down on a pang of guilt. "I didn't get you exiled," I said. "Fuck, Anya, I barely knew what that meant. I never wanted this job, you know; you were the one who started asking me for favours."

"And you got what you asked for in return."

"Bullshit." Anger spiked deep in my stomach, boiling up out of the guilt. "I didn't know."

Anya shrugged and disappeared into the kitchen, giving me the time to compose myself. When she came back she was carrying two coffees on a tray, milk in its own jug and old-fashioned sugar cubes piled up on a plate. She put it down and curled up on the armchair, legs tucked beneath her. "You wanted it," she said. "We needed someone with talent and connections to keep things secret; the job was there for the taking and you showed up to take it, whether you know that or not. You'll have to accept that, one of these days. You were made for this, Miriam Aster, the fey and everything else. You adapted too well for it to be otherwise." She smiled at me, her lips tight. My coffee cup hovered around my chin as I wondered whether I should be throwing the hot liquid in her face. I didn't; Anya always had good coffee and I needed the kick more than I needed petty satisfaction.

"I don't want to rehash the past," I said. "I just need some information. You had fingerprints all over that crime scene."

"Fingerprints?" She smiled, cocky, and fluttered her fingers. "We don't leave prints, remember?"

"You know what I mean." I scratched the back of my neck and sniffed, watching her reaction. She sipped her coffee.

"I can't help you on this one, Aster."

"Right." I put the coffee cup down, fighting the temptation to really let loose. "Anya Titan, fairy scholar extraordinaire, queen in fucking exile, the woman who closed the great gate to Fearie. Are you really telling me you don't know *anything?*"

"There are other scholars," she said. She looked away, just like the photo on her dust jacket. "And there are others who could tell you what you need to know."

"Yeah, there are," I said. "But I know you, you're the best, and you still fucking owe me a favour. I'm not looking to cut a new deal here, Anya. Your people don't give anything without taking something in return, and I'm sick of playing that game. That's why I walked, remember?"

I fidgeted in the awkward silence that followed. Anya didn't. "There are rules," she said. "Even for us, even after we leave it behind. That means there are consequences, just like last time." She looked at me with clear, violet eyes; those changeling eyes that were green as emeralds when we first met, gray as gunmetal during the years we spent together. "Are you ready for that, Aster? Is it really that important?"

"I've lived through consequences before." I scratched at my chest, just below the collar. Her blush was like watching the sun rise. "There were ghost-memories, Anya, clear as anything. One minute I'm looking through a crime scene and then all I can see is you and me together. I trust that, and it's your fault I trust that. If you don't want to help me, then I'm fairly certain someone else is setting it up. Someone wanted me to come here, and it sure as hell wasn't me."

"Talk to one of the others." She stood, headed for her bureau. I watched her pull a pencil out of a drawer and go searching for some paper. "I can give you a list. Reputable academics, other exiles with a grudge, the usual type you'll need."

"I'm still a virgin," I said, keeping my voice low. Anya froze, turned, and a small smile crept across her face.

"I seem to remember that part a little differently," she said. She gave me a look and I felt the quick thrill of a younger woman's desire. I scowled at her until the smile faded. "Untouched by man," I said. "That's what you always told me, and fucked up and archaic as the definition is, that's all it takes when dealing with your kind. I'm still a virgin, Anya. In every way that counts to your folk, I'm still considered pure. I could compel you, if I wanted to. You taught me that."

"And you'd do it?"

I shrugged. "If that's what it takes. She was just a girl. She deserved better than a gutful of fairy spawn and a long sleep in a dumpster. I don't have time to wait for the white horse to knock up some other kid, and I can't risk a plague of pure-blood fey swarming across the city. So yeah, I'd compel you, if it came down to that."

I waited, letting the silence work on her. Eventually she nodded. "Hobb" she said. "The gates closed, but there are back ways, secret ways through. He's the only one going back and forth these days, the only one who'd even have access to a unicorn. Go find him and compel him to get your answers."

I stood up and drained my mug. "Thanks for the coffee," I said. Anya didn't look at me, just watched the black grounds floating across the surface of her untouched drink. I headed for the door and let myself out. She came after me while I lingered in the hall. "Aster," she said. I stopped walking, but I didn't turn around. "If you need me," Anya said. She tripped over the rest of the words, took a deep breath and forced them out. "Do what you need to do, okay. For old times' sake, for that last favour, I've got your back on this one."

My stomach went cold, but I nodded. I went down to my car and took a couple of long, deep breaths before I started it up.

CHAPTER 4

In theory I was going home to sleep, the job should have been over once I got Kesey his lead. I phoned through to his desk at the precinct, rattled off Hobb's description and a list of known haunts while Kesey took notes on the other end. When I was done I poured myself a fresh gin and nursed it in bed, still wearing my suit as I crawled under the covers. Nothing I'd done since telling Heath to burn Sally Crown's corpse was going to do a damn thing to stop the unicorn – Kesey would put out a BOLO on Hobb, setting the uniforms on the search for guys matching his description while Homicide tried to chase down a paper trail. The fact that Hobb barely left one wouldn't matter to Tim; it's what you did when you were looking for suspects, fey or no fey. Maybe they'd get lucky and find him before sunset, but odds were they didn't have the resources to hold him. My gut said another body would turn up full of spawn before anyone on the Force got the job done. I knew Hobb, had worked with him a couple of times doing favours for Anya, had worked against him as many times yet. It was going to take more than cops on the lookout and good luck to catch up with him.

It had barely gone six-thirty when I rolled out of bed and geared up, ditching the suit for something comfortable and swapping out the steel caps for sneakers. Heavy boots made a great impression when standing my ground against someone like

Kesey, but this time I planned on running from any trouble. I could handle myself, if it came to it, but when you're working alone and without backup, discretion is always the smarter fucking choice. I loaded up on the usual barter tools – spare cash, hipflasks, a pair of brass knuckles – and unlocked the safe in the bottom drawer where I kept the revolver.

Do a search of my flat and you'll find plenty of guns, all of them neatly locked away despite the message sent by the piles of clothes and dirty dishes. Working Homicide makes you nervous at the best of times, and nothing I'd seen since the days I left the force did anything to dissuade me when it came to being armed.

I had a lot of guns, but there was only one revolver, an archaic chunk of blue metal with as few moving parts as I could get away with and still have it fire a bullet. There was nothing special about the gun, but I understood how it worked. Clean parts, a basic mechanism; science I could understand. Ten years back I'd trained with it every week, getting used to the heavy kick and the strange pull of the custom ammo that I'd commissioned two cities over so it was less likely to be traced. Since then it'd been locked away, a private insurance policy I assumed I'd never use again.

Outside, the city was winding into action, sunrise drawing out the first signs of traffic. I got changed in my cramped bathroom, ignoring the scars when I looked into the mirror. Jeans, a black t-shirt, my favourite jacket.

"You really going to do this?" The jacket was bulky, the fabric heavy enough to swamp my figure and give the illusion of mass across the shoulders. It was a habit I'd picked up when I still worked Homicide, fighting the macho pricks in my department to get cases and respect. It was Kesey who taught me the trick after I first got out of uniform; mass is a weapon when you're dealing with the old boys club, a threat you can throw around if you've got the guts or the chops to back it up. It wasn't a pretty look, but it did the job. I slid the revolver into a pocket, checked the bulge to make sure it wasn't too obvious. I stared at my reflection. "Right, then."

I left.

. . .

The stone cold truth about fey is this: they're a race of goddamned parasites. I can list you a whole mess of reasons why I don't like getting involved in their business, some of which are personal and some commonsense, but that's the reason that sits at the heart of all the others. Once upon a time they fed on belief, and there's enough people out there with Tinkerbell on their t-shirts to make me think they still do. But a fey cut off from Faerie is left with limited options. Exiled fey tend to run low on juice unless they're drawing power from something else; some emotion that's raw and human and easy to soak in.

Hobb liked older women, single and a little desperate. Knowing his habits made him easier to track, and I'd seen his charm in action enough times that I knew what to look for. I wasn't immune, but I could put a bullet in his arm the moment he tried something and that'd work well enough.

The rain hit as I drove down to Chalke Street. It was one of those places that didn't look right during daylight, all those dull and dead neon lights hanging forlornly over the footpath. I pulled up in an empty space and sat for a while, the rain splattering the windshield. Just coming up on breakfast and the street was still crowded, the last remnants of the dusk-to-dawn party kids stumbling out of the clubs and heading off into the dreary morning. Most of them were happy to stumble through the downpour, dancing in the streets as the rain bounced off the pavement. I lit a cigarette and waited, not bothering to be inconspicuous; I drove a Chrysler Sigma I'd picked up cheap, a rusting car built around hard, black angles that stood out against the wet light of morning. I turned the stereo off and listened to the rain rattling on the roof.

Hobb appeared right on nine o'clock, splashing down the footpath with a woman nestled under his arm. She was middle-aged and crumpled, the sharp cut of her business suit turned shabby by the rain and the night of carousing with a hobgoblin. He looked like one of those guys you see from time to time, too damned ugly to have landed even a rumpled woman like her, but somehow capable of making it work. You could write it off as confidence, but it took more than that. Hobb was a twisted stump of a man with a lecher's grin and a teenager's hubris. He sang as he walked, swinging a wine bottle in his free hand. His date was holding him upright, sagging a little under his weight. I wound down the window.

"Hobb." My voice wasn't loud enough to carry through the rain, but Hobb's head snapped sideways regardless. His beady little eyes locked onto the car, glinted red and green as he blinked against the water. His date stumbled as he halted. The wine bottle shattered against the concrete.

"Miriam Aster, I'll-be-fucking-damned," Hobb said. He untangled himself and crept forward, leaning over to stare through the open window. He took care to hover, not touching the car door. Rainwater ran down his face, causing the pockmarks to gleam. "I thought we were done with you. Should have known we weren't that lucky." I dug a cheap, plastic hipflask out of my jacket pocket and waved it in his face. Hobb licked his lips, fingers flexing. "What do you want, Aster? It's raining, and I've got places to be."

He flicked a glance over his shoulder, towards the giggling woman, and I shook my head. "Ditch the girl, Hobb. You and I need to talk." Hobb sneered, giving me an eyeful of the sharp teeth he hid behind his lips. I gave him a cold smile for his effort. "Now."

"Bitch," he said, but staggered over to the girl and whispered something into her ear. I watched her body language change, stiffening, her eyes glazing over like he'd just fed her a roofie. Hobb staggered around to the far side of the car. I opened the door and he slumped into the passenger seat. "It's been a long time, Aster. You going to give me that flask or what?"

I flipped the hipflask into his lap and watched him scramble at it, gulping the bourbon in a long, smooth motion. He finished with a satisfied sigh, licking his lips with a pale tongue that reminded me of a slug. "So, what the fuck do you want?"

"Information," I said. "There's a unicorn on the loose, in

heat and dangerous. It's already killed its first virgin." Hobb flashed me the teeth again, passing the flask back.

"Bully for the white horse," he said. "Nothing to do with me, though. I'm not responsible, not this time."

"Bullshit." Hobb cocked his head to one side and stared at me, examining me with mismatched eyes; one blue, one grey, both too large for his squashed features. His hand strayed for the doorhandle, skittered along the metal handle. He was cornered and he knew it. "People have pointed me at you," I said, "and I'll compel you if I have to."

Hobb laughed. "You've been out of the game too long, Aster. No-one compels me, remember? 'Specially not a two-bit ex-cop who retains her virginity on a technicality. It's a loophole, m'dear, and I'm the master of loopholes. You can compel me all you want, but it ain't gonna do a damn shit. Perhaps you should go chat with Her Majesty again, ask her to point fingers in another direction. Hell, maybe you should just ask her for a target, get her vengeance all fired up and go marching off into the night. You liked being her instrument last time, gunning someone down on her say-so. Maybe you liked it a little too much?" I flinched and Hobb belched. The car filled with a stench like rotting fish. "I bet that hurt, going to see her, after all the trouble she caused. Did she tell you she loved you, again?" His laughter turned into a cackle, a horrid sound that echoed above than the rain-rattle on the roof. I pulled the revolver out of my right pocket and pointed it at him. His nostrils flared as he caught the scent, the laughter going dead as his eyes went wide.

"Raw iron," I said. My voice was calm. "They'll hurt like hell, even if it isn't enough to kill you. Tell me about the unicorn, Hobb."

"I don't know nothing." Words tumbled out of his mouth, rushing after one another as his eyes locked onto the gun barrel. "Honest, Aster, I didn't do anything. I heard some rumours that folks were selling the horn-horses, but that's it. I don't know who they're selling to, and I don't know who did the selling." He whimpered and shrank back against the car door, leapt forward again as the metal bit into him. His eyes watered. I watched him for a long time, then nodded and put the gun away. Hobb started clawing for the door handle.

"If you're lying," I said.

"I'm not," Hobb said. "I swear, Aster. I swear." I leaned over and opened the car door. Hobb scrambled into the rain, leaving his date behind as he disappeared into the downpour.

I gave him a twenty count and went after him. You spend enough time around fey, even exiles like Hobb and Anya, and you get used to hearing half-truths and outright lies every time they open their mouths. You don't question a guy like Hobb to get answers, you question him to get him panicking and hope he leads you somewhere useful. Years on the Force had taught me that much, and working with Hobb had proved its value more than once. I watched him scurry down the street, fleeing into the wet dawn like a frightened deer. I abandoned the car and followed him on foot. Hobb was short and fast, graceful in a way that didn't fit his twisted frame. I lumbered along behind him, wincing every time I heard the wet slap of my sneakers on the pavement.

Tailing someone properly takes two people and it works better if the guy you're following doesn't know you. I was alone and Hobb could ID me on sight; in theory it should've been difficult to tail him, but whether you're a fairy or not, a drunk is still a drunk. If you scare them, they drink to cope. Hobb was half-gone when we started, kept drinking as we walked. I stayed a few blocks back, kept him in sight as he stumbled his way towards a strip club on the river.

It was one of those hole-in-the-wall places, access via a cramped alley with loose bricks in the wall and bad lighting. He knocked for maybe a minute before the door swung open and a solid lump of bouncer emerged. I wasn't close enough to hear the conversation, but the buzz of Hobb's quick sentences echoed for a moment before he disappeared inside.

I retreated to a bus stop across the street, watched the flashing neon sign bolted into the brickwork. It lost impact in the daylight, but it still had a dim glow in the shadows of the alleyway. I snapped a shot of the sign with the camera in my phone: *The Hot House*. I knew the place. It was bad news but it wasn't usually a hangout for guys like Hobb. I contemplated calling Kesey in, doing it by the book, but suspicion didn't make for a search warrant and Hobb didn't exactly exist in city records anyway. I was still in the process of deciding my next move when someone stepped behind me and pressed a gun into my back.

"Waiting for a bus, miss?" It was a soft, slithering kind of voice, deadly as a sniper-shot.

"Waiting for a friend, actually."

A hand clamped down on my shoulder, pulling me upwards. The gun barrel in my back didn't move. "Maybe he's inside," the voice said. The hand on my shoulder drifted down to my jacket pocket, removing the revolver. "You and me, we should take a look."

He pushed, urging me forward. I went; it seemed safer than arguing.

CHAPTER 5

It was a short walk down the alleyway and the gun never wavered. If the bouncers noticed me coming up to the entrance at gunpoint they didn't make a show of it. We were waved through, quick and easy, the quiet menace of the gunman always behind my right shoulder.

The Hot House had a morning shift, but it wasn't the kind of place that drew a large crowd, just a small group of dedicated perverts. The club smelt of desperation, a sick reek of stale sweat and whisky that seemed perverse given the early hour. There was a teenage girl on stage, throwing herself about to a disco beat and staring down the audience with a bored expression that seemed to dare the patrons to watch her. I spotted a handful of dockworkers: fresh, big men looking for a place to have a stiff drink and wind down after work before heading home to crash. The rest of the patrons were the same fringe dwelling nightmares you find lingering in any bar that's open after sunrise. The gun at my back disappeared, but the hand clamped down on my shoulder clawed me hard enough to leave a bruise.

"Sit," the voice said, and pushed me down onto a bar stool next to a black plastic table. "Hands where we can see them, okay?" I put both hands on the tabletop. It was sticky and unpleasant. The soft voice sat down next to me, one hand disappearing into a menacingly full pocket. He was thin and sharp, like a whip crack given form. "Call me Slick," he said, raising his voice just loud enough to compete with the thump of the music. "I'll be your babysitter til Mister Drabble is done talking to your friend."

He nodded to the far side of the room where Hobb sat talking to a man in a black suit, a cadaverous rake with oversized eyes that threatened to pop out of his face as he stared at the stage show. Hobb sat next to him, drink in hand, talking fast as Mister Drabble watched the show. Drabble was flanked by a bodyguard, a slab of meat built for some serious looming. Hobb kept throwing nervous glances at the meat-slab, flinching whenever he tossed a glare in my direction. Drabble looked bored. I stared at him, hoping for some sign that he was fey, but Drabble and his boys seemed dangerously mundane.

"Shouldn't stare," Slick hissed. "It makes Mister Drabble nervous." His eyes flicked over me, lingering on my chest. They narrowed to dangerous slits and he smiled. "You have pretty hair. You should grow it out. It'd make you look like a lady instead of a dyke."

I didn't dignify that with a response, and Slick let loose a tinny laugh. The music changed, picking up pace. The girl onstage finished her dance and another one came out, dressed up like a schoolgirl with braces on her teeth. Mister Drabble held up a hand to stop Hobb's rambling and nodded to his bodyguard. The slab of meat lumbered over. He moved like a boxer that'd taken a couple of shots too many, his right lip busted open and already starting to crust. "Boss'll see you," he slurred, and helped Slick get me to my feet. Together they hustled me towards Drabble's table, sat me down and held me in place while Drabble ignored my presence. Hobb gave me a smug smile, leaned across and whispered in my ear. "Fuck you, Aster. You shoulda known better than to try following me."

Drabble hissed, soft and sharp, and Hobb drew back, cowed into submission. That wasn't a good sign. Slick turned his attention to Hobb, giving him the evil eye. Drabble's attention was locked on the schoolgirl, ignoring all of us. It wasn't until the music thumped to a halt and she skipped offstage that he turned to face me, his leer drooping.

"Well, what are we doing with you?" He had a high voice, a whiner's voice. "You're too old to work here, love, and too plain to do well in any of my other places. That doesn't leave us with too many options." He smiled, showing off a mouth full of teeth straight out of a soap opera, white and perfect. His breath stank of peppermint.

"I already have a job," I said. "I'm looking for a unicorn."

Drabble laughed. "Well, you won't find one here, love," he said. "But maybe we could find you a horn or two, if you're willing to give the boys a show." He grinned a little, rallying behind the joke as he looked me over. "Then again, maybe not."

"Not interested in horn," I told him. "Not unless it's attached to the horse."

Drabble's eyes narrowed, dangerous and angry. "So what's your name, love?"

"Aster," I said. "Freelance detective."

"Not what Hobb here says. He says you're a cop. Told us all about you."

"Used to be, when Hobb and I first met," I shrugged. "But that was then. Freelance investigation pays better."

Hobb snickered, leaning forward to whisper in Mister Drabble's ear. Drabble's smile was all thick teeth and minty menace. "Freelance is dangerous work, isn't it? No backup, no check-ins, no law to protect you if things go wrong. Perhaps you should just fuck off, used-to-be-a-cop Aster, and forget all this bullshit they got you looking into. Not worth it, yeah? You're better off taking another job."

I looked around the empty club, the small crowd and the skeleton staff, a new girl doing a half-hearted bump and grind on stage. "'Fraid I can't," I said. "There's a unicorn in heat out there. Hobb knows what that means, but I'm guessing he hasn't told you. It isn't pretty, Drabble. Fuck it, it's more trouble than you can handle."

I was pressing buttons, trying to get him riled up. Drabble didn't take the bait. "I said fuck off, love. I can get Vin and Slick to kick you out, if that makes it easier. Look elsewhere for your white horse, and leave Mister Hobb out of your investigation. Do you understand me, Miss Aster?"

I stood up, keeping my hands visible. Hobb grinned at me, smug. "Obviously we had a misunderstanding," I said. "Sorry for the inconvenience." I started towards the door. Vin and Slick dropped into position beside me, hands on my shoulders. It was smart positioning, professional; get behind someone and they can bolt for freedom, but they closed down my angles and left me nowhere to go except the way they wanted me too.

They didn't want me going out the front door, and I knew right then that there was going to be trouble.

They pressed me against the door of a black Ford Falcon while Vin patted me down, his busted lip twisting into a smirk whenever he started pushing his hands somewhere private. He had a boxer's hands for sure, great paws with malformed knuckles, large enough to squish my head like a grape. He wasn't built to do anything gently; by the time he hustled me into the back seat I was covered in bruises.

I didn't recognise the driver but Slick sat in the passenger seat, a pomaded madman in a cheap suit who grinned as Vin manhandled me. Slick held a Beretta in a loose grip, the steel black and oily against the pale pink of his manicured hands. He had my revolver in his other hand, flipped it open and emptied a bullet into his palm. He gave it a quick sniff, grinning. I sat still, hands on my lap, waiting for them to give me a move I could make without ending up dead. Vin handed my ID over and Slick read the details as the Ford started and drifted along the dock roads, cruising like we weren't really going anywhere important.

"Interesting ammo," he said, eyes flicking over my license. "Wouldn't have thought of that, me."

"I like to be prepared," I said. A smile tugged at the edges of his mouth. He folded my ID back into the wallet and tossed it into my lap.

"Just like a fucking boy scout," he said. "Would have cost you a bundle, getting them done up like that, making sure they work. Custom job. Very pretty. D'ya mind if I keep them?"

"I'd prefer to have them back," I said. "As you said, they cost a bundle. I'd hate to fork out that much cash again." Vin coughed, choking on his laughter. Slick gave me a dirty grin, spun the chamber on my revolver and flicked his wrist a second later, clicking it into place. "Mister Drabble wants you dead," he said. "The runt says killing you is a mistake. That you've got friends who can make life miserable."

"Maybe," I said. "I used to be a cop and all. Someone on the Force still likes me."

"The runt ain't talking about friends on the Force," Slick said. "The runt is talkin' about *special* friends, friends like him. Says they'll raise your ghost and send it after us if we kill you, all death curses and vengeance."

"He could have a point, there," I said. "I've been dead once before, after all."

Slick pushed at the collar of my t-shirt with the barrel of his gun, stretched it far enough to see the scar. "So the runt said."

The car took a tight corner, wheels hissing on the wet road. The sharp turn tipped Slick off-balance and he dropped the gun down as he steadied himself. I let the momentum carry me sidewise, the point of my elbow caught Vin in the ribs. He grunted, sprawling against the door as my weight crashed into him. As moves go, it was pretty weak, but I wasn't going to have any other opportunities.

I pushed upright, one hand reaching for the door, and came eye-to-barrel with Slick's gun. I blinked and forced myself to look past the gun, to stare Slick down. He had brown eyes, both of them the same shade.

"I like to be prepared too," Slick said. "Remember that."

Vin's chest was heaving as he tried to breath again, his big body shaking against the door. Slick stared me down, the gun never wavering. "Kill you or don't kill you," he said. "I don't much care either way, Miriam Aster, but I'm a pragmatist at heart. The boss gives me the job and I do it, no questions, no complaints. If you come back, well, I guess that just means we have to keep on killing you, again and again, until it takes." He pulled back on the pistol, chambering a round. The Ford pulled up on the riverbank, a deserted car park surrounded by warehouses. Slick weighed my revolver in his off hand, as though trying to make up his mind which to use. "Iron bullets," he said, shaking his head. "Really, it's like you think you're hunting werewolves."

"Silver," I said. Slick cocked his head. "It's silver for werewolves."

Slicks eyes reduced to slits. "Funny thing, you having bullets like this. The runt said you used to work with him, playing nice with the fairies. Said that you used to bump uglies with some kind of queen."

"Used to. Past tense," I said. "She wasn't a queen then, either."

That earned me a smile that gave me chills. "Runt said I should check that, if I was gonna kill you," Slick said. He shook his head, adopting a rueful expression with all the sincerity of a bad actor. "You could have been a nice looking woman. Pity."

Vin pushed me out of the car and lined me up on the riverbank. It was a short drop to the rocky shore and the dark water. In the end Slick went with his Berretta. I heard the sharp crack, the sting of something hitting me right under the collar. I was still conscious enough to hear the second shot, but I was gone before the pain registered, disappearing into the white light and the soothing calm.

I fell back, twisting. I don't remember hitting the ground.

CHAPTER 6

I know what it's like to be dead, and I'm not a fan of the experience. The saving grace is that you don't remember all of it afterwards, just little bits and pieces that come back to you in flashes. You're dead, you know you're dead, but it feels like a dream. There's a bullet hole in your chest and nothing hurts, which is how you can tell it's for real. You're dead, kind-of; maybe not quite dead enough to go wherever you're supposed to, but it's close enough for horseshoes. Close enough for the morgue and a scalpel and the bag-and-tag of your organs.

The bits that I remember go something like this:

I'm back at the club where we first met, a hole-in-the-wall that smells of cigarette smoke and beer. I smell her before I see her, sweet and tender as honeysuckle. She's tall and proud. Her eyes don't match. She's a femme. Not my type, not really, but it's enough to get me interested. She wasn't Anya-fucking-Titan then, not yet. She walks towards me and sits down. She asks me for my name. I tell her. She buys me a drink. I buy one for her. I'm still a uniform, just starting to angle for detective. She seems interested in my job. A few hours later she lets me take her home.

I'm walking down Carmody Street with my arm around Anya; six months since our first date and everything's going good. We're celebrating my promotion, talking and laughing, our bellies full of Korma and beer, my fingers slowly inching their way towards the nape of her neck. Anya plays with my hair, boy-short and spiked, a little too extreme for my colleagues on the Force. "I love you," she whispers. I shake my head. "No, you don't," I tell her. "Loving me is a very bad idea." And I'm right, we both know I'm right, but sometimes the brain doesn't pass those messages on and my body is young and stupid and too in love to care. When Anya kisses me, I kiss back. She hooks an arm around the small of my back. I purr. She pulls my hand to hers, holding it against the curve of my belly. She holds tight, possessive, like I'm going to run away. We cut down the alleyway behind the Indian restaurant. "You shouldn't be a cop," Anya says. "It's dangerous; there are dangerous people out there, and worse things besides." We're in the alley. We find the corpse of Sally Crown, facedown in the dumpster, her blue-white body covered with fairy dust and her broken tiara shattered against the concrete. "I can keep you safe," Anya says. "If you say you love me, I can keep you safe from harm."

That last time we saw each other, on the steps of her apartment. I've shot a man, killed him, on Anya's say-so, her anger ringing in my ears as I pulled the trigger. She tells me she loves me. It's the last time I let her do that. I'm burned out and afraid. My career is over. I don't want to do favours for her anymore.

"I don't want to love you," I tell her. I'm lying through my teeth.

"That doesn't mean you don't," Anya says.

"It doesn't mean that I do either."

Anya smiles. Her eyes sparkle. "That's close enough."

She kisses me again. She tastes like lavender. "I can help," she tells me. "Let me help, okay?"

There's blood spilling out of my shoulder wound. Even more spilling out of the hole in my chest.

I woke up in the morgue, lying flat on Heath's autopsy table. My chest ached, the kind of pain that comes with broken ribs and displaced organs. My shoulder ached, a purple mess, flesh battered like a heavyweight's punching bag and a fresh bullet scar just below the collarbone. Heath hovered beside the table, reading a magazine, long hair dangling over his eyes. I moaned and he raised an eyebrow. "You went to see her again, didn't you?" The sticky sensation of drying blood and river water clung to me despite the pre-autopsy clean-up. I breathed in, my first real breath in a few hours, and I caught Anya's scent in the air. It felt good to breathe, normal. Heath let out a short sigh of relief. "Fuck, Aster. Kesey's going to be pissed."

"Time?" My voice was an urgent mouse-squeak, still weak and raw. "How long?"

"About a day." Heath's face appeared in my field of vision, a little blurry around the edges. "You were the only job tonight, if that's what you're wondering. No need for the furnace. Not yet."

I sat up, twisting my shoulder to stretch out some of the pain. Keith had draped me in a spare shirt from his office, left it dangling open and undone. My numb fingers fumbled with the plastic buttons, trying to close it up. Eventually I gave up; there were stitches in my chest again, so it wasn't like I was hiding anything. Modesty seemed stupid after Heath had removed and weighed my lungs. "Another fucking autopsy?"

My stomach rolled. The novelty of breathing wore off and I noticed how my lungs hurt. I coughed up dry blood, spat it into a tray Heath shoved in front of me. He put it down amongst the scalpels, secateurs and rib-spreaders. I wiped my mouth with the back of my sleeve. Heath threw me a jacket and I pulled it on, shivering.

"I didn't think you were coming back from this one." Heath shook a steel tray and two bullets rattled inside it. "And I wanted the bullets."

"Forceps," I croaked. The stitches in my chest stung, but they hurt far less than they should have done. I was healing fast, but that would end soon enough. "Pull them out like I'm an injured person."

"It's not like you'll notice another scar."

"I notice the first one, Heath. Trust me, I'll notice a second."

"She didn't call to tell me." He looked away, embarrassed.

"Hell, Miriam, I didn't think she still had the power to do something like this. Not without, you know…"

"I don't love her."

"You're back from the dead," Heath said. "She's an exile. She doesn't have that kind of power anymore, not on her own."

"We're taking her word on that," I said. I lay back on the slab, closing my eyes. My head hurt. "I don't love her, Heath. Not anymore."

"Yet here you are." He handed me a cigarette and lit it. "So. Kesey?"

"I was thinking we didn't need to tell him."

"You were shot." Heath rolled his eyes, slapping both hands on the slab. "Hell, you were D.O.A, Aster. Homicide cops tend to hear about that, and you know he was waiting for this the moment you signed up for the case."

"Kesey doesn't want to know," I said. "You wouldn't have a job if he did. Neither would I."

"Even Kesey has limits."

That was true enough, and I figured we were coming up against them fast. "Get the slugs to the lab." My hands were steadier, so I tried my shirt again. "They come from a nine millimetre carried by an arsehole named Slick, works for some big shot who runs a club by the river — the Hot House — a guy named Drabble. It'll keep Kesey distracted."

"The strip joint?" Heath's grin went snarky. "I thought you were looking for a unicorn."

"Fuck you too," I said. I could stand up, but my legs were shaky. Heath had to help me through the first few steps. I lit a second cigarette, trying to drown out the taste of being dead. "I need a drink," I said. "What you got?"

"Coffee, tea, half a bottle of scotch and some beer."

"That'll do for starters," I said. "Start with the tar and use the scotch for flavour. We'll get to the beer soon enough."

We drank. Whatever magic had me back together after Heath had cut me open left me feeling anxious, and the whisky took the edge off the discomfort of my internal organs settling back into their proper places. When Heath suggested going home and getting some sleep I sent him out for more beer instead. "Death's sobering," I told him. "I'm drinking my way back to normalcy."

He wasn't happy about it, but he went. I marked it up as an improvement. The last time I died he'd insisted on checking me into a hospital and the questions the doctors asked got awkward. The morgue was empty in his absence, the cold room devoid of new deliveries. It made me nervous. A unicorn in heat wasn't stopping at one victim, so there'd be another body showing up before the night was over. I thought about ringing Anya and decided against it. It was bad enough, owing her a favour this big again. I didn't want to talk about it. Instead I made a list of the various ways I was going to take last night out on Hobb's hide when I found him.

By the time Heath came back I was puking up blood, making a mess of the sink in his office and clawing at the stitches in my chest. He made a point of ignoring the tears, just cleaned me up and handed me a fresh beer. "You should get some sleep," he said. "Sooner or later."

I didn't much feel like it. "Last time I didn't lie down for three days. Hell, I barely even sleep anymore. Bad dreams."

"You can't just wait around for a body, Aster. And you can't run on booze and fumes."

"I'm not. I'm thinking." I drank my beer. "On a scale of one-to-ten, Heath, on a scale like that, what's the odds that Her Majesty knew nothing about this?"

Heath looked away, hiding behind his fringe. He opened a beer. "I don't know her that well," he said. "It's just phonecalls, favours. Don't ask, don't tell."

"What's your gut say?" I glared at him, forcing him to answer. It took a while before he broke.

"Pretty good," he said. "On a scale of one-to-ten, I figure the odds are pretty good."

I hauled back on the dregs of my beer, my stomach churning. "Me too," I said. "Fuck it." I wobbled back over to the sink and let loose. Eventually I passed out and he set me up on a couch in the foyer.

I didn't wake up until four am when my phone started

blaring in my ear. The hangover was there already, a sharp headache and a queasy feeling that wasn't just caused by liquor. Heath had given me a lab coat as a blanket but I was still cold and shivering. I checked the display and saw Kesey's name written in block capitals. I groaned, answered it anyway. "Yeah?"

"Get moving," he said. "We found a new body."

CHAPTER 7

Twenty minutes later I was back on the waterfront, not far from where Slick had dumped my body the day before. You couldn't miss the cop cars, the yellow tape stretched out to mark off the empty stretch of shore. My stitches itched like crazy. I scratched and smelt lilac on my fingers, the tell-tale stink of magic. Bored uniforms swarmed along the police line, protecting the crime scene from the occasional seagull. One of them recognised me from the search at the alley, waved me through before the others could ask for ID. I ducked under the tape and wandered in, weaving through the yellow spotlights and their whining generators. The light was cold and clinical, filling the crime scene with long shadows. No sign of Kesey, but there was a team setting up a winch by the riverbank. I ambled over and took a look.

The corpse lying in the mud might have been the unicorn we were looking for, but it'd seen better days. There was pale blood spread across the unicorn's forehead, just below the pale stump that used to be a spiralling ivory horn. Black mud streaked the dead beast's fur, soaking in like ink stains. Heath was a pig in shit, merrily prodding and poking his way through a virgin crime scene. I stood at the top of the riverbank, trying not to throw up, trying not to shudder when I saw the revolver sunk into the mud next to the corpse. "What you got?"

Heath turned and looked up, squinting into the long shadow

I cast under the spotlights. "Iron bullets," he said. "Someone wanted the damn thing dead. No track marks through the mud, so I figure someone just dumped the body over the edge." He stood up and cocked his head to one side. "Know many people who carry cast iron bullets in their gun, Aster?"

I ignored him. "Where's Kesey?"

"Out interviewing locals." Heath shrugged and went back to his corpse. "You know Tim. He hates seeing this shit up close. He's not open-minded and adaptable like you and me."

"That's because you're both freaks." Kesey appeared out of the darkness, lurching up and looking over my shoulder. He let out a slow breath between the gaps in his teeth. "So that's a unicorn," he said.

"Not quite, but it's close."

"What's the difference?"

"About twelve inches of horn and a mean look in its eye," I said. "Someone did a number on the poor bastard."

Kesey gave me a look, trying to work out if I was kidding. "You look like shit," he said.

"I had a rough night. You can ask Heath for the details, if you really want to know."

He looked away, studying the skyline. "Do I want to know?"

"Shit, Tim, *I'd* rather not know."

"Damn." He folded his arms, blinked a few times as though that would change the scene. "*Damn it*. I really didn't want to believe in this shit." He walked back to the police line and I tagged along behind him. I offered him a cigarette as soon as we were clear.

"The unicorn's dead, you can let this slide now."

Kesey stared, trying to read my face. "I guess you're done then," he said. "I'll clear your fee in the morning and leave it with Heath. You can pick up the cheque at the morgue."

I cleared my throat. "When they run ballistics on the bullets in the horse, they're going to be from my gun." I said. Kesey kept his cool better than I was expecting, but the veins still popped in his neck. "I got a lead last night; a guy named Drabble at a club called The Hot House. It was one of his boys who roughed me up and took the gun. Dollars to donuts he's mixed up in this, somehow."

"Tony Drabble?"

"You know the name?"

Kesey grunted. "Small time thug turned big time entrepreneur. I'm sure you remember the type."

"Trailed Hobb to his club, they're up to something together. His boys had a go at me when they realised I was there on business."

"You were supposed to be advising."

"I was. I am."

Kesey sighed. "We'll need more than that to move on Drabble. He has lawyers, these days."

"Fuck, Tim, *you* need more than that." My right hand scratched at my chest, right above the scar from the bullet, then went to work on the stitches. "This guys a bastard and I'm not quite as burdened by the need for hard evidence these days. Call it the joys of working freelance."

"You aren't working freelance," Kesey said. "You're working for us."

"I'm a consultant," I said, grinning at him. "I figure I stopped the moment the unicorn was found and I confirmed you had your killer. Unless you're planning on going after whoever put the bullets into the white horse, I figure we're done."

Kesey shook his head. "Christ, you used to be a cop, Aster. A good one."

"I used to be a lot of things," I told him. "These days, I'm a little more pragmatic."

Kesey turned on me, giving me one of his famous looks, dark eyes blazing with barely controlled anger. The man was fifty-six and hard, the kind of detective they used to terrify raw rookies, but I was a little more jaded than I'd been back when we first met. I smoked my cigarette down to the filter and watched as they hauled the corpse up the steep incline. "You don't get to do this one by the book, Kesey," I said. "A rogue unicorn, that's one thing. A rogue unicorn showing up dead, that's something else. You've basically got two options; you pin this on me when the ballistics report comes in and pretend it never happened, or you go after the bastard responsible before he tries bringing in something that's even worse."

Kesey simmered, trying to stay in control. "You got an alibi if I try the first option?"

"I was busy being dead," I said. "As alibis go it could be difficult to prove in court, but Heath's resourceful and I'm confident he's up to the challenge." I dropped my cigarette and stomped on it. "Tell me about Drabble. You said he worked small."

"He did, once upon a time," Kesey said. "Now he's your basic sleazebag success story; turned one club into a small chain. Got big into computers, I think; runs a dozen porn sites, uses the money for less legit business when he needs too. Vice wants him taken down, but Drabble's got lawyers upon lawyers these days. His own little army of trained attack dogs with degrees. We don't even get him to trial."

"What's he doing with a unicorn, then?"

"Aster, I don't even fucking know what I'm doing talking about one." Kesey closed his eyes and leaned back, turning his face to the night sky. "Hell, I don't even want the damn thing to exist."

He took a deep breath. "I think you're done on this," he said. "The unicorn's gone, so we play it like we should. We get Drabble for a real crime, none of this fairy shit, and we take him down proper."

I nodded. "If you're sure."

"I'm sure," Kesey said, "Leave it. Don't go looking for a problem that isn't there."

I took it as good an excuse as any to go home and catch up on sleep.

Kesey cut me a cheque the next day. I picked it up and went drinking, blotting out twenty-four hours so I didn't have to think about the job or Sally Crown or whatever the fuck Hobb and Drabble were doing with that unicorn. *It's dead*, I told myself. *No unicorn, no case. The citizens are safe and no one's paying you to keep on poking.* I dreamt of Anya. I didn't go and see her. I spent a few fruitless days trying to track down Hobb, but the runt had gone to ground. I drank more to pass the time.

I was still drinking a week later when Heath called me and told me to drop by the morgue. "It's about that last consult," he said. "Kind of. I think. You'll want to see this. Not want, I guess, but-"

I wasn't in the mood. "What, you found something during the autopsy on the horse?"

"Not quite." Heath sounded choked up and lost. "Just, come down, okay. I need to show you something. You need to see it."

He hung up on me. Heath wasn't one for hanging up on someone, and given his proclivities I didn't want to think about whatever had him rattled. I ignored his second phonecall, and the third, but the calls didn't stop and eventually I agreed to meet him.

I took my time getting to the morgue and did the usual procrastination I always did before heading inside. Heath didn't wait for me, just walked out to the parking lot with his white coat pulled tight while I was finishing my cigarette. "Sally Crown," he said. "I lost her goddamn records, Aster. I incinerated her body and pretended it never happened." He pushed a photograph of Sally into my hands, her dead face serene as she lay on the slab. "We shouldn't have let this one go. She was a kid. Her parents still think she's missing."

"I didn't think you were one to care, Heath."

"I talked to her," he said. He wasn't talking about Sally anymore.

"Your call," I said. "But I'm done with the job. No more unicorn, no more Anya. Kesey officially called it closed and I got paid for consulting. I got rent to pay, Heath. You know that."

"It's not that easy, Aster." He fished a DVD case out of his pocket and gave it to me. His hands were shaking, and he looked a little green. "I had to give a copy of this to Kesey," Heath said. "Had to, you got that? He's in the loop on this one, whether you want him to be or not. He didn't want you having a copy of it, but, you know, I just thought, I guess, that you should know."

I opened the case and looked at the disc inside, a silver circle with the case number written across it in Heath's jittery handwriting. "What the hell is it?"

"Just, you know, watch it," Heath said. "It's an internet thing. People have been posting it around on the fringe porn sites, real sick fuckers, you know? A friend mentioned it to me and, well ... I had to pay a couple hundred bucks to get a copy, all under the table shit. And when you watch it ... listen, I want these people taken down, yeah? You work with Kesey and you take them down, right?"

"Sure."

"I asked her," he said. "I mean, there are favours and there are favours, yeah? She says she didn't know about this one, Aster. She promised. She swore."

Heath lingered for a moment, his eyes locked on the disc. I raised an eyebrow at him, but he turned away. "Don't watch it on a full stomach," he said. "Trust me, just don't."

CHAPTER 8

I fed the DVD into my computer. It took a couple of seconds to pull up the file — video, no file name, just a string of numbers. I double clicked and watched the footage bloom to life, a grainy shot of a girl's bedroom done up like a doll's house. The colours were washed out, but you could see lace and feathers and the frilly curtains over the windows.

The camera focused in on a red-headed woman, her right hand slowly working the unicorn's horn with a fistful of Vaseline. The beast nickered, rolling its eyes back in pleasure, its expression too inhuman to be fake. Somewhere behind the camera someone yelled, "You ready love? Okay. Action," and the fluffer disappeared off to the right side of the shot. My breathing stopped when the camera scrolled across, focused in on the naked girl in the background. She was sprawled out on the edge of the bed, face lost amidst a burst of static as the camera refocused. The unicorn's horn shone, radiant in the spotlight. I could see rainbows playing off the slick surface as it approached the bed. I watched the horn lower, teasing the flesh of her inner thigh, gently forcing the girl's legs to separate. "No," I said, but the horn slipped in, penetrating the soft fold between her legs with a single, slow thrust.

I try to forget that video, but I can't. The camera glides in. Close up. Close enough to show the cornsilk hair, the green eyes, the plastic tiara covered in glitter. The face of Sally Crown without the stain of rigor mortis. Her features contort. She gives the camera a theatrical gasp. The horn furrows between her legs. A real gasp, the sharp point digging into sensitive flesh. She screams, her voice filled with pain, and the unicorn's horn starts pushing deeper and deeper.

I could hear the director's voice off-camera, still giving orders, taking it for granted that he'll be edited out in post-production. No-one onscreen is listening to him; beauty and the beast are already beyond the possibility of control. I paused the video, leaned in, recognised the gleam of lust and madness in the unicorn's eyes. "Shit."

I hit play and Sally started screaming again. It takes too long for the crew to recognise the difference between her fake cries and the real ones. I could hear them muttering, a blur of voices behind the camera. I got up, knocking over my chair. The horn forced its way deeper; squelching. The unicorn raised its head, lifting Sally. More memories that don't go away. She bounces, impaled, a china doll taped to the head of a hobby-horse. The computer speakers fill with screaming; a deep voice yelling directions, ordering the unicorn to stop; someone else calling for a tranquiliser, anything to put the unicorn down. Sally Crown screams and screams and screams, tears flowing. She's caught. The unicorn bobs and thrusts. Sally flails, trying to push free. The horn too deep for her to escape.

It all ends with a wet pop, and Sally Crown is a dead balloon. The unicorn lowers its head, scrapes her limp form free, holds its bloody horn high in triumph. A gunshot, a feathered dart in its flank, the quick spin as it glares at someone standing behind the camera. The unicorn lowers its head and charges. The camera-shot spins, rushing past the crew. I see a flash of familiar, too-white teeth before it tumbles to the floor. Somewhere behind the lens there's screaming, a director yelling orders, the sound of another gunshot. The camera fixed, at its odd fallen angle, on the blank face of Sally Crown. I stare at the screen, willing her to move, ignoring the muffled thump of hooves. Then the shot dissolves, disappearing into a cloud of static. Eventually I got up and ejected the DVD, snapping the shiny plastic in two. I contemplated the bathroom, but rage ran roughshod over the desire to throw up. I called Kesey.

"You watched it? Heath's movie?"

"Yes."

"I want in," I said. "When you're taking the bastard down, I want in."

"You're a consultant, Aster. You don't take people down, not on something as big as this."

"Tim—" I said. He cut me off.

"No. You advised, you got paid, now you leave this to the professionals. We let you handle things your way last time, Miriam. I can't afford to let you do it again. We can take him on normal charges, the unicorn won't be mentioned."

"You can make it stick?"

"We'll have to." Kesey's voice was cold and serious. "This goes down clean and legal, Aster. No favours for your friends, no letting things slide, no hiding the truth when someone gets shot resisting arrest."

"I can help. I want to help."

"You're not a cop, Miriam," Kesey said. "If you were, I'd let you handle this in a second, but you made that call ten years ago. There's no way in hell you're coming in on this."

I told him to go fuck himself and hung up. Then I drove over to Westbury, a gun in my jacket pocket.

She was standing in her doorway as I hit the top of the stairs, a scarecrow in a black jacket that didn't quite fit her shoulders anymore. I stormed towards her, trying to look threatening. She knew it was bullshit immediately; if I hadn't hit her during our breakup, I wasn't going to start now.

"Come in," Anya said. "I'll make tea."

She looked withered, dishevelled in a way I'd never seen her. I looked just as bad; I'd been crying on the way over, but the tears were gone, only the salt smear on my cheeks remained. "You look like shit," I said.

She gave me a wan smile. "Thanks. Sit."

I sat and watched her go through the fastidious ritual of making tea, the slow accumulation of loose leaves and a copper kettle and stove-boiled water. She moved slower now, her gestures less precise. Magic, I guessed. It would've taken a lot out of her, bringing me back. There were rules about it, big ones. "The unicorn's dead," I said. "They found it by the river."

She paused, hands on the side of the stove. The kettle sat on the hotplate, steam rising out of its spout. "Who did it?"

I shrugged. "I don't know for sure, but there was a guy named Drabble. He was behind it, working with Hobb. They took the horn after it was dead."

Anya's face twisted. She coughed, covering her mouth with one hand. "I'm sorry," she said. She didn't turn around. "Was it bad?"

I said nothing, waiting for her to look at me. When she gave in, I nodded. "It was bad."

"But you stopped it?" Her voice was a whisper, her eyes wide. Anya tended to play sorrow like a pantomime actor, but I knew her well enough to know that part of this was real.

"No," I said. "I haven't."

The kettle whistled while she stared at me, trying to read my expression. I closed myself down, kept the anger huddled below the surface, waiting. We were in familiar ground now, just like old times. She removed the kettle without looking at it, her eyes locked on mine.

"I want answers," I said. "The right ones, this time. Did you know?"

"Know?"

"The unicorn. What they were doing."

She had the grace to blush, her cheeks turning a dusty rose, but she didn't look away. Anya didn't do contrition any better than she did sorrow. "No."

"But you knew it was here?"

"Yes."

"And you helped Hobb get it here, from the other side?" She

busied herself with the tea, refusing to answer. I shook my head. "Figures."

Anya looked up at me, hands still, her face calm. "So what happens now?"

"The law," I said. "Kesey's got a warrant and a hard on to take Drabble down. It'll probably happen, if the State lawyers are any good."

"Probably?" Anya cocked her head to one side, staring at me like a bird. She lifted the kettle onto a wooden tray, arranged cups from the row on her windowsill.

"The unicorn presents a problem," I said. "Kesey wants to take Drabble down for underage porn, but there's nothing on the books about unicorns and minors, and Drabble has good lawyers. He'll go away, but there's no chance it'll be for as long as he deserves."

Anya sat the tray down on the coffee table, pouring tea. "You're not happy."

"No," I said. "I'm not. The fucker should be dead."

She handed me a cup and dropped two sugar cubes into the brown liquid. "Aster, do you still love me?"

"Does it matter?"

"Sometimes." She blinked, her eyes misting up. "Sometimes it matters more than anything."

"Why?"

Anya stood up, letting her long hair flare out behind her like a pair of wings. She stared down at me, eyes bright with urgent desire. She'd gotten herself exiled for me, way back when, that first time she brought me back from the dead. It took a lot more out of her this time, but she was still too damn pretty. Still too fucking beautiful. "You're a virgin," she said.

I shook my head. "That's a stupid rule."

"We didn't make it." Anya stared at me, her eyes blazing. "It's all about belief for my kind, Aster, and men made the rules when they took over the culture. It's never meant that much to us, gender, but your people think otherwise."

"It's a technicality," I said. "You know that better than anyone."

"You're a virgin," she repeated. "In every way that matters to the magic of my kind. We can destroy him, if you wish it. Annihilate him and make him pay. The curse of a fey is a powerful thing, even when it's uttered by an exile like me. Ask me, and I can do it."

I blinked. We'd gone that route before, and it hadn't worked out. Anya stood, waiting, her body thrumming with power. "You knew," I said. "You were lying before. You knew what he was doing."

Anya nodded. "Not at first, but eventually. I moved to stop it."

I lit a cigarette, watched the irritation flash across her face. "A girl died. Sally Crown. You could have stopped it earlier."

"It's not like it was, Aster. I don't have that kind of power, not without-"

"Bullshit."

"It's true," she said. "Hobb did what he did. I want him to pay for it. But it takes time, now. I can't just give an order."

"You asked for me, when Heath called about the girl. You wanted me on this." This time she paused, face caught in a flicker of hesitation, but she nodded.

"I needed help." Anya reached out, put her hand on my arm. "Love is a powerful thing, in the hands of the fey."

I grabbed her hand and lifted it off my forearm. I didn't trust myself to leave it there. I leaned in, close enough that my cigarette smoke rose up into her face. "You don't love me, Anya. You use me."

She withdrew, stung, and I checked my watch. "Here's how it will go from here," I said. "Kesey will have raids stationed to hit every warehouse and club on Drabble's books. They'll hit them simultaneously, right on dawn. Whole teams of heavily armed, shotgun wielding cops will go through everything Drabble owns with fine-toothed combs looking for the concrete proof they need to put Drabble away. Kesey will play it by the book. He'll keep the unicorn out of it. Tony Drabble will be tried by a jury of his peers and rot in jail. Eventually he'll die, old and lonely and behind bars. You'll be safe. Hobb too, probably, if he's smart enough to clear out once the cops move in."

Anya picked up her teacup and stared into it. "That's not enough, is it."

"No. It never is."

"I'm sorry, Miriam." It was her first apology. The first I remembered, anyway.

"I don't want you to be sorry." I stubbed my cigarette out on my saucer. "I want you to be useful."

"You know the price," Anya said. She touched me again, hand on my chest. Her fingers traced the ridge of the autopsy scar under my shirt. "All you need to do is ask."

"I don't love you," I said.

"Yes," she whispered. "You do."

"I don't want to."

She smiled at me. "That's not the same thing."

"No." I took a deep breath and stared into her eyes, one gold and the other green. I thought about Sally Crown, just ashes in the morgue furnace now, another missing persons case that no-one will ever solve. "I guess it's not. But I heard it was close enough."

Anya's smile was eager and terrible. "I could destroy them for you," she said. "It doesn't have to be like last time. They hurt you, and I could curse them. If you say you love me I could demand vengeance for your wounds."

"I don't want you to curse them, I just want you to find them. Give me a location and let me handle the destruction." For a moment Anya's expression was blank. Then it wasn't. Something hungry showed up in her eyes; hell hath no fury like a queen-in-exile scorned. She'd expected it to be like the old days and it hurt bad now she'd realised it wasn't. I clenched my fist, ready to play hardball.

"Just do it," I said. "I'm still a fucking virgin and I'm fucking compelling you. Fucking do it. Do your thing and tell me where."

She dipped her finger in her tea, face twisted up in anger. Damp fingertips traced a sign across my forehead, and she leant forward to kiss my eyes. The touch of her lips was far from pleasant. "I make you my instrument and give you the gift of vengeance," she said, her words winding around me, tight and powerful. "Until you find the man who slew you, and the man who gave the order. Fare thee well, beloved."

I closed my eyes and I could feel them, Slick and Drabble. They were a weight in the corner of my mind, a presence as easy to read as a compass point. I could feel an echo of Anya's anger too, her burning need to hurt Hobb and Drabble and anyone else in my way. It pushed against me, hungry for blood. I pushed back, taking steady breaths until the rage was bottled up and corked, ready to explode when I needed it.

"Miriam." Anya's breath brushed my face. I opened my eyes and looked at her. "When you find them ... I need the horn," she said.

I rolled my eyes. "Of course you do."

"It's too dangerous to leave out there." Anya pulled back. "There's too many things it can be used for, none of them good. It should be returned back where it belongs. I don't know if you can get it, but if you can—"

"Don't." I stepped in and kissed her, long and slow. "Just wish me luck."

Anya nodded, eyes shining. I went downstairs and climbed into the Sigma. I pulled the spare gun from my jacket pocket and checked the clip. Ordinary bullets for this one, but they'd do the job nicely on a sleaze like Drabble. They were to the north, out past the suburbs. I could feel the distance like a sixth sense, a twenty minute drive. I checked my watch. It'd take them another hour to get the warrants signed, even longer before the raids were in place. Even if Kesey and his men knew where to find them, it'd be enough time to get there before them.

I gunned the engine and drove, disappearing into the night.

CHAPTER 9

I drove north, following the highway out into the hinterlands, up into the smaller estates where the rich folks used to live before the hills were filled with roaming fey and people abandoned the area for less temperamental dwellings. We may have burned the permanent paths between earth and fairy, but there were still enough woods out here to ensure fairy circles grew in the light of the full moon. There were still ways through, if you were willing to look for them. Anya's kiss lay heavy on my eyelids, pulling me forward. I took a turnoff onto a narrow country road, threading through small estates and villas that overlooked the city. I looked behind me using the rear view, watching the city sparkle in the crisp night air, a shadowy mass lit up by twinkling streetlights. My gut said I shouldn't be out here, so far from the light and backup and the cops Kesey had working the case. I ignored it and followed the pull, turning down a poorly paved driveway that cut through the woods.

When my gut said I was getting close, I killed the engine and continued on foot, following the curve of the long driveway from the edge of the woods. The night air smelled of pine trees and I could hear small things scampering in the undergrowth. I wrote most of them off as insects and vermin, but odds were some of them weren't, this far out. It was a full moon, light enough to see by. There was a ditch between the driveway and the tree line, a narrow gulch full of shadows. The gun in my hand felt heavy, but it was a comfortable weight. I followed the ditch until I found Drabble's place, a decaying husk of a faux-Tuscan villa in stained white brick and terracotta tile. Slick and Vin were standing guard at the front gate and an eager need to hurt them leapt up inside me, urging me to lead with the gun. I kept to the shadows, forcing myself to stay calm. I crept forward, sneakers squelching against the damp grass. Slick was smoking, looking idle. Vin scanned the road, watching for headlights, but he didn't seem to have noticed me skulking along in the darkness.

I stepped out, gun held steady in a standing grip. I had to breathe steady, force myself not to pull the trigger. "Hi," I said. "Do me a favour, boys; fish the armaments out of your pockets, one after the other, and toss them towards the trees. You aren't my favourite people right now, so don't think I won't shoot you if I have to."

It was a stupid move when faced with two shooters, but people who think you're dead tend to hesitate when they see you again, especially when you've got a gun. Anya's vengeance was like a drug. It made me reckless.

Vin gaped at me, his eyes darting wildly as he tried to process my presence. Slick just smiled. "Welcome back, Miss Aster," he said. "Did you find your white horse?"

"She a ghost, Slick?" Vin whispered, *sotto voce*, as though I might not hear. I fired a warning shot and he got the idea, reaching inside his jacket and pulling out a heavy .45 that thumped into the grass when he threw it aside. Slick didn't make a move, didn't even give Vin an answer.

"I was meaning to ask, Miss Aster, last time we met. What's it like to be dead?"

"Cold," I said. "My turn: where's my revolver?"

"Inside," Slick said. "Mister Drabble has it, along with the horn. Some kind of insurance policy, I think, while he works out what to do with the little runt." He cocked his head to one side, his eyes cold and flat in the moonlight. "You planning on shooting me?"

"Can't say I haven't thought about it," I said. "You planning on giving me a reason to?"

"Like I said, Miss Aster, I'm a pragmatist. The boss says do a job, I do it. Questions just get in the way."

"You coming back from the dead if I shoot you, Slick?"

"It's a neat trick." He shook himself, loosening his shoulders. "Not to my taste. I don't like the cold."

Vin lost his nerve at that, roaring towards me with an ugly expression. I could hear his heavy boots crunching against the tiled drive as I fired and caught him twice in the chest. It did nothing to slow him down and Vin crashed over me like a wave, crushing me to the ground. I kept hold of my .38 as I went, tried to fight my way free by slamming the butt of the gun against the side of Vin's head. I could hear the steady huff of his breath as he swung at me, meaty fists hammering at my face, but he didn't have the angle for a solid strike. I knew Slick was armed without even looking at him, the tingling sixth sense of Anya's vengeance marking him, making him as easy to sense as a spare appendage. I kicked free of Vin and rolled away just before Slick started shooting. Vin screamed as I scrambled for the cover of the ditch, the pain of the gunshots finally hitting him. He staggered to his feet and caught a stray bullet from Slick, blood fountaining out of his right arm. Slick kept shooting, bullets sliding past me and cracking as they impacted wood. I fired blind as I scrambled, loose shots over my shoulder that were guided by vengeance and instinct. Slick rewarded me with a long hiss of pain and a soft clank as he fell back against the bars of the gate. I took a peek over my shoulder, saw Slick pushing himself upright, bleeding from a wound to the hip. The Barretta in his fist weaved a lazy arc as he scanned the darkness. Vin whimpered, a quivering mess of muscle and bloodloss on the ground between us.

I stood up. Slick snapped off a wild shot and I caught him in the stomach, leaving him to scream while I took deep breaths and watched the gun spill out of his hand. I walked over, lowered my weapon, pushed his Berretta away with my toe. Vin whimpered as I kicked down with my heel, snapping his skull into the tiled driveway with enough force to shut him up. Slick's breathing was ragged, blood flecking his lip in the moonlight.

"Pretty hair," he said, then there was nothing but the gate and house lights and the slow chirp of the crickets reasserting themselves in the sudden silence.

I went over the gate, feet searching for purchase on the iron bars, blunt spikes bruising my stomach muscles as I swung over the top. I watched as the lights in the villa went out, one by one, an obvious precaution given the sound of gunfire. The darkness didn't bother me. I kept off the path, coming up to the house through the yard, using the trees for cover. I could feel Drabble's presence upstairs, the weight of it dragging on me like I was a fish caught on a line. I gave the front door a wide berth, picking the lock on a side window and rolling into a powder-pink bathroom.

Drabble's house smelt like baby powder. The rooms were bare, scattered with the shadowy silhouette of a few random pieces of furniture. My sneakers squeaked on the hardwood, the sound echoing against the walls. I moved through the murky darkness, gun out, ears straining. I started working my way from room to room, letting instinct take over. The furniture was all cheap and easy to clean, the rooms always arranged so there were beds and broad couches squashed against the far wall. Cheap video cameras sat dormant on flimsy tripods, pointing towards the furniture. Apart from that, the lower floor was empty. There was only one main staircase leading to the upper level. I was expecting a small barrage of gunfire when I tried it, but there was only a single muzzle-flash as I scoped out the upper landing.

Hobb's voice came out of the darkness. "I told him it wouldn't be enough to kill you, Aster." He giggled a crazy laugh. "You and Her Majesty, you've still got a thing going, even if you don't want to admit it." He was perched on the railing, curled up with one long arm wrapped around his knees, his mismatched eyes watching me as I peered around the corner. Drabble was lurking further back in the shadows, gun in hand. I could see the moonlight playing off the barrel.

I dropped back behind the cover of a candy cane coloured wall. "Hey Hobb," I said. "Just so you know, I'm not letting you off for this one."

Hobb's laughter spiralled out of control, his small frame rocking on the banister. It was a brazen position, arrogant, but he knew that Drabble had my revolver and there wasn't much I could do to hurt him with the peashooter in my hand. "I don't get 'let off', Aster," he said. "I get forgiven for the unfortunate things I do in the name of duty. Poor little Miriam, you still don't get it, even after all these years."

"It's just you and me and a sleazebag with a thing for little girls," I said. "Who, exactly, is going to forgive you, Hobb? You should have been holed up here with an army of thugs, but you aren't. Drabble's still small time really. Still doesn't think anyone's coming for him unless they're the law, hasn't prepared for the possibility of someone coming in here all crazy and-"

"Shut up." Drabble took a step forward, the gun steady in his hand. "You should come out, love, or things are going to get messy."

"Fuck you," I said. I leaned out, just a little, and let off a quick shot. Drabble shot first, soon as he saw the movement, and a chunk of plaster disappeared just beside my head. "We saw the tape, Drabble. The cops are raiding everything you own, freezing your accounts. You're fucked, and you know it."

Drabble fired another round. I heard it thump into the wood-panel wall just a few feet from my hiding space. "The cops aren't here, love," he whispered. "You think we didn't hear about the raid? This place is off the books. Safe. Just the way the crew likes it. Just the way the clients like it. There's just you and the two of us. Hobb figures if we kill you again, you'll stay dead for good this time."

I heard Hobb snickering. "It's true, Aster. Dead for good, this time. Her Majesty hasn't got the juice for another stunt like that, not on the scraps of affection you've been feeding her."

"It's not about affection anymore, Hobb," I said. "This time I'm here to exact Anya's vengeances. It seems she's pissed about what you've been up to and she needed someone to relay her displeasure." The implications were lost on Drabble, but Hobb's laughter cut short. I heard him slip off the banister, feet scuffing against the floor.

"Bullshit," he said. "You doing her bidding again? After all this time?" I stuck an arm around the corner and fired blind. I heard wood splintering, heard Hobb swearing under his breath.

"No bullshit, Hobb," I said. I fired another shot. Drabble fired back. "She wants both of you punished, wants you living a fate worse than death. I'm just here for the mercy killing of the sucker you lured into this."

They whispered, falling back. I listened to their footsteps work their way across the upper floor. I took the stairs slow, slapped a fresh clip into the gun. Hobb was chanting in the darkness, doing his best to counter the effects of Anya's magic. I felt the link to Drabble wane, dribbling away until his presence was like an unscratched itch. There was blood in the upstairs hall; I'd winged one of them. Not dripping fast enough to leave a trail, but I swung right and trusted my luck to hold, worked my way past the doorways one by one, going right door to left and scanning. Long shadows filled the rooms, the hall lit up by the full moon filtering through the skylight.

I found Hobb first, cowering in a bathroom. Everything was cold moonlight through the window and soft shadows on the tile. His shoulder was bleeding, but he didn't seem to notice. He launched himself at me with his hands spread, going for my neck. I slammed the gun into the bridge of his nose and watched him flail backwards, falling against the sink. His breathing was wet and blood smeared the lower half of his face. Hobb whimpered, letting loose a stream of muffled "fucks". I put a bullet in his stomach and another in his leg. Lead shot, not iron; he'd heal fast enough, but he wasn't going to be running anywhere for a day or two. I felt Drabble come up behind me a split second too late, heard the soft click of his gun echoing against the tile walls. "Drop the gun," he whined. "Get your hands up, love."

I put the gun on the side of the sink and turned, hands kept out in the open. Drabble flicked the light in the bathroom and I blinked, blinded, as he reached out and snagged the automatic.

"It was never meant to happen," Drabble said. "That girl and the horse, it was never meant to happen. Hobb said it was safe."

"Hobb lies," I said. "It's his one great talent in life. A unicorn in heat has the self control of a two-year–old."

Drabble tucked my gun into his waistband, next to a length of white horn and my revolver. He backed out of the room and motioned me forward. The other gun stayed locked on my stomach, his hand steady as he adjusted the .38. His smile was unpleasant as I stepped into the hall. "You should have left it, love," he said. "We cleaned up after ourselves, we got rid of the horse when it got out of control." He patted the horn at his belt. "Alive or dead, the damn thing was still going to make us a profit. Nobody got hurt except that girl, and who the fuck cares about another teenage runaway?"

He stepped forward, covering me with the gun, getting ready to shove me towards the stairs. I couldn't sense him like before, but I could feel the burning need of Anya's vengeance running through me. I watched him, anger rising up in my eyes. Drabble met my gaze, stumbled, and his gun hand wavered a few inches. I clenched a fist and swung, catching the side of his head. I followed up with a knee to the crotch. Drabble went sideways, face twisting in pain, gun skittering down the hall. I dashed for it, diving and rolling aside. He was upright, drawing my revolver from his waistband. I threw my weight sideways and pulled the trigger. The house echoed with the sound of gunshots. Drabble bled from the gut, folding over as he dropped forward. My arm was stinging, slick with blood. I pushed myself up using the wall and walked over, covering him the whole way. My head pounded, pushing me forward. I put the barrel of the gun to his head.

"You pissed off the wrong woman," I said, and I could feel Anya's cool fingers over mine, urging me to pull the trigger. "The vengeance of a fey is a powerful thing." There was still enough of Drabble not yet in pain that he wet himself at the prospect of what could come next.

"Here's how it's going to go," I said and I hammered a knee into his jaw and felt something break beneath the impact. Drabble went face first into the carpet, bleeding and broken, but he was still breathing through the mess I'd made of his face. "You're going to be tried, you're going to be convicted, and you're going to spend the rest of your life wishing I'd damn well killed you."

Hobb was gone, slipped out the window while Drabble and I were busy shooting holes in one another. I thought about going after him, decided against it. I slipped the horn out of Drabble's belt and tucked it into my jacket. Then I fished my phone out and called Kesey to come clean up the mess.

CHAPTER 10

I hadn't killed him and Anya's magic made sure that hurt every moment I sat there watching him bleed over the floor. Drabble sucked in wet breaths for a half-hour before Kesey and his boys arrived. He bled a lot, but he survived long enough for an ambulance crew to handcuff him to a gurney and drag him off under an armed escort. He'd spend a couple of weeks in hospital, but he'd heal up fine for the court dates and Kesey had found enough hard evidence that even Drabble's team of legal pitbulls wasn't going to be able to do shit for him. I sat on the front step of the house, letting a paramedic bandage up my arm, ignoring his suggestions that I go to a hospital to have it checked out. I patted down my jacket with my free hand, looking for cigarettes. Kesey offered me one of his instead. I took it, lit up, and watched the ambulance cart Drabble away.

"We would have got him," Kesey said. He sat down beside me, cigarette dangling from his thick fingers. I winced as the bandage went on. I'd taken two shots to the same shoulder in as many days. It was starting to get old but at least this time around the bullet had missed anything vital. "You weren't even advising on this one, Aster. I should take away your fucking license."

I shrugged and watched the ambulance disappear through the gates, past the white sheets covering Slick and Vin and the team snapping photographs and taking sketches of the bodies. "So you had this place covered then," I said. "Your crack team was lying in wait, ready to rescue my arse if things got hairy?"

"We would have got him," Kesey repeated.

"As long as you got a case against him," I said. "One that doesn't involve that footage."

Kesey didn't say anything, he just sat there and finished his cigarette. When he was done, he patted my good shoulder and stood up, heading inside to supervise the team working the scene upstairs. It was the closest thing to approval I was going to get out of him. I waited until he disappeared through the front door before I called after him.

"Hey, Kesey," I said, and he reappeared. "Say hello to your sister for me, next time you see her." The smile vanished and he disappeared again. I got one of the blue-and-whites to drive me home, took a handful of painkillers to dull the pain before I went to sleep.

I found Hobb in a Chinese restaurant three weeks later using his charm to impress the waitresses as he consumed vast amounts of food and imported Chinese beer. He was eating alone, so I slipped into the booth on the opposite side of his table and slipped the revolver out of my pocket before he recognised me through the alcoholic haze. Rumour had it he'd been drinking hard since Drabble went down, so it took him a moment to process. Even drunk, I figured I wouldn't have found him if he hadn't wanted to be found.

"Miriam Aster," he said. He belched and I could smell sweet and sour sauce on his breath. "About fucking time."

"Hey Hobb," I said. I picked up a fork with my free hand and speared some honey chicken off his plate. His ugly face twisted up as he squinted at me, swaying in place. "You here to kill me, Aster?"

"If I wanted you dead, I'd have let you finish your meal. The food here is terrible."

He rolled his eyes. "The waitresses are cute. What more do you want?"

"I've been thinking," I said. "Ten years back, when I was involved with Anya, you used to work for her, right?" Hobb nodded, and I leaned in to make sure I had his attention. "I want to know when you stopped."

Hobb belched again, and this time it smelled so foul the smell sent me backwards. It stank like mulch, like something rotting in his gut. He patted his belly in the aftermath, grinning like a jack o'lantern. "Officially? I never stopped. A queen of the fey in exile is still, after all, a queen. I may have pushed things a little … further than expected … this time around, but she'll forgive me. Eventually. It's what she does." He took a long slug of beer and winced, covered it up by squinting at me. "How's your work, at present, after all this unpleasantness?"

"Good," I said, and it was only partly a lie. Kesey pulled my license for review, just like he'd threatened to. He wasn't happy about it, but he wasn't unhappy either. There was a second cheque waiting for me for the consultancy on Drabble's capture, paying me for the time put in after the unicorn was found. It was enough to last me a month or two, and I wasn't worried about work. Even if they took the license away for my shootout with Drabble, they'd reinstate me as soon as they needed someone to consult on the next bout of weird shit that rolled through Heath's morgue. "I'm taking a short sabbatical. Letting the injuries heal."

A waitress with chopsticks in her hair bustled past, asking if I'd like to order. I gave her a few bucks and asked for a pot of tea, hoping like hell it wasn't as bad as the food. Hobb blinked at me a few times, as though trying to fix on my face. I'd never seen him truly drunk before, despite his copious drinking. He sweated badly. "Listen," he said, "just ask."

"Ask what?"

"Did she know about the unicorn? Why did she agree to help? Whatever question about Her Majesty that's got you showing up here, being polite, when we both know you want to break all my toes and fingers. We aren't friends, Aster, and I'm running out of time and patience; be rude. Ask."

"Why'd she help you?" I asked. "After all the trouble the last one caused, why'd she help you bring another unicorn in?"

Hobb's smile showed off a wide half-moon of yellowing teeth. "Because she knows you, Miriam Aster. If there was a unicorn, you'd get involved. You may have bundled yourself up in guilt and denial, but you can't help yourself when the trouble starts. Eventually you'd investigate, and eventually you'd go see her, and in her heart of hearts Her Majesty still wants you back."

It was a smart-arse answer, or maybe it wasn't, but either way I hauled myself across the table and slugged him for it. It didn't do much beyond making him laugh, but it made me feel better to have done it all the same.

They found Hobb dead a few days later, facedown in his beer at a bar along the strip. No bullet wounds, no evidence of foul play, just dead and a little bloated from three straight days of drinking. I'm guessing he rotted away, from the inside out. Anya was pissed at him, and I wasn't much for believing her when she claimed she didn't have the power to take care of one of her own. Kesey asked me to answer some questions when they found the corpse, but I begged off on that one. All I had were some lucky guesses and they were probably wrong.

Anya left messages on my answering machine for weeks, twice a day while the trial went public. I didn't call her back. I got a phonecall from Heath about a month after they put Drabble away, asking me to meet him for a coffee. Part of me wanted to say no, but Heath was the golden goose to my fucked up little business. It didn't pay to piss him off.

It felt weird going out for coffee; Heath and I weren't coffee kind of people and the place he picked was tragic. A murky, behind-closed-doors kind of attitude with carefully crafted ambiance straight out of a spy movie. He was waiting for me when I arrived, habitually late and pissed off. "Miriam," he said, waving me over from the door. "How's the shoulder holding up?"

It hurt, still, but it was okay. The wounds were scars now, my arm just a little stiff after the injuries it'd sustained. I had a second crease on my chest, one running either side of my belly button. I punched him in the shoulder to prove I was in working condition and ordered an espresso. "What do you want Heath?"

"She's been calling the morgue," Heath said. He blushed as he said it, knowing I'd be pissed. I'd never seen Heath blush; I'd prefer to avoid a repeat of the experience. "Not often, but checking up. She asked me to ditch some files, the autopsy on that Hobb guy, and she asked me how you were doing. Asked if I knew what happened to the horn they cut off the white horse before they killed it."

"And?" I said. "What, you're looking for advice?" Heath shook his head.

"I told her I didn't know," he said. "And that you were on holidays, just like you said. She sounded worried, Aster. I just figured you should know."

Our coffees came, hot and steaming. I drank mine without saying anything, and Heath squirmed as he tried to fill the silence with inane chatter and gossip. I watched his eyes, one a little greener than the other. He looked different outside the confines of the morgue, a little less sallow around the edges. "She's disappointed I didn't kill him," I said. "She wanted the fucker dead, just like she took care of Hobb."

Heath stopped talking, mouth left open. He shrugged and looked into his coffee. "I don't know," he said. "Me, I just figure, if she wanted him dead, he'd be dead, you know? She doesn't seem like the kind of woman who fucks around when she wants something."

I grunted and dropped a couple of bucks on the table. Then I pulled a brown paper package about twelve-inches long out of my pocket and dropped it next to the change. "I'm going home," I said. "Next time they need a troubleshooter, tell Anya to find someone else."

Heath stared at the package for a moment. "You should call her back," Heath said. "Fuck, Aster, she saved your life."

He'd give it back to her, probably. I didn't much care if he didn't. It was a cold morning outside the café, cold enough to make the scars ache. "Yeah," I said. "I guess she did at that."

He didn't mention it again. I left.

BLEED

CHAPTER 1

The first rule Walt Colton ever taught me about dealing with the fey was simple: *when a faerie asks you to kill someone, the worst thing you can say is "sure."* Only fucking idiots let a faerie manipulate them like that. The fey hate hard and they hate fucking long and once you've let them saddle you with a fragment of that anger it treats the interior of your skull like an echo chamber and hammers away until the killing's done. The only way to deal with faeries, the only way that's safe, is to make yourself numb. Anything else and they'll mess you up.

The second rule he taught me was *never fall in love with a faerie*, but I didn't listen to him on that one either.

It was after five and I was sitting in Colton's joint, filling in some of my copious free time with a few glasses of medicinal gin. It wasn't really my kind of place; a small, second-storey bar where everything reeked of money. Hardwood floors, mahogany Furniture, a handcrafted counter imported from France. Not the kind place you bought on an honest cop's retirement fund, but I try not to let that bother me. I don't have so many old friends that I can afford to alienate the ones left.

My name's Miriam Aster and I used to be an honest cop myself, but that rep went south with the rest of my career a good ten years back. These days I work freelance, if there's work to be done, and the gin fills in the rest of the time with a pleasing kind of numbness. I'd spent the last week working hard on the latter, trying to quiet the bourgeoning headache ready to bloom behind my right eyeball. Pain's one of those things you get used to when you break Colton's first rule, especially when you leave the job half-finished and walk away.

I was starting on my third drink when Colton nudged my arm. He was a big guy, well-dressed. You wouldn't pick him as an ex-cop, but that's not exactly surprising. Colton ran in different circles to most of us even in the old days, and he'd learnt the art of staying beneath the radar. He tilted his head towards the door. "You've got a visitor, love."

I shook my head. Nothing good ever came of that phrase. "Tell 'em to piss off," I said. "I'm on sabbatical."

Walt stared at the doorway for a second, his face impassive. "Don't think she's leaving."

I glanced over my shoulder and spotted Safia Mulani. She was standing by the glass door, watching me, waiting. One hand scrubbed through her short, dark hair and she tried a nervous grin. I turned back to the arsehole in the emerald cravat pouring my next gin. "This your doing, Walter?"

Walt's shrug was surprisingly graceful for his size. "Consider it one of the problems with having a local, love. People know how to find you."

I snorted into the remnants of my drink. "This isn't my local, Walt. My local is dingier and they make me pay for drinks."

"I can fix one of those, if you need me too."

I raised an eyebrow at him, but Walt's face stayed neutral. He placed a fresh drink in front of me. I picked up the glass and took a long slug, letting the gin hit the back of my throat without really tasting it. "You're a bastard, Walt."

"Sure I am, but I'm the bastard on your side." He made a point of adjusting his cravat, flashing a cheesy smile across the room. "Hear her out, at least. You owe her that much."

I leant back a little, stared at him. "I will shoot you, you know that, right?"

"Your call," Walt said. "Me, I'd listen to her, if you know what I mean." He rapped a knuckle against his forehead and winked at me. I hated it when he did that. There's nothing worse than a prescient bastard with a habit of meddling, even if he is on your side.

"Five minutes," I said. "She gets five fucking minutes, then I walk."

Walt waved Safia over, a grin forming beneath his moustache. "Whatever you say, love. Whatever you say."

I glared at him. Walt had a dirty mind, but nothing ever happened between Safia Mulani and me. We'd met a few years after my trouble with the faeries, during the period where Colton hooked me up as security for one of the local production companies. The Mulani twins were American imports, an actress and stuntwoman combo willing to be the big fish in our small local pond. Six weeks after I worked overnight security on one of Safia's stunt riggings, her sister disappeared while they were shooting in bushland.

After I started doing freelance investigations, Safia became a client but the situation never lasted long. Bad things happen when I work for women I'm attracted to, and I liked Safia too much to let my shit seep into her world. So I tried to stay away, to put some reasonable replacement on her sister's case. It never seemed to work for long. Every few years she'd show up, toting some new clue about her sister's disappearance, and I'd forget to say "no" until the same trouble started up and reminded me why I stayed away.

She settled onto the stool next to mine, her leather jacket creaking as she leant her elbows against the bar. "You're looking well," she said.

I tried to ignore her, but the sweet lemony scent of her perfume crowded me and demanded my attention. Safia looked good. Short and solid, her shoulders built with sleek muscle. Walt found something important to do at the far end of the bar, leaving the two of us alone.

Safia nudged my arm. "This is the part where you say something."

"Fuck," I said.

"More than that, maybe. I'm not here to give you grief, Miriam." Safia smiled, trying to set me at ease.

It didn't work. "What do you want, Saf?"

"The same thing as always. I need your help."

I focused my attention on the gin, savouring the taste this time round. Walt was right when he said I owed her but that didn't bother me much. I owe a lot of people and I've grown used to disappointing them over the years. "Not going to happen," I said. "I thought I was clear about that, after the last time."

She put a hand on my forearm. Just rested it there, easy. "You were. I'm asking anyway."

I gave in and looked at her, studied the sharp lines of her face. Her beauty was stark and functional, like the sharp-edged glamour of a straight razor under a bright light. A curved scar beneath her right eye contrasted with her coffee-toned skin, the legacy of a stunt gone wrong.

"Talk fast," I said, tapping my drink. "I'm out of here once this is done with."

A thin smile marred her lips. "Harry Peaseblossom."

"Don't know him."

Her smile wilted. "You're sure?"

"Very." I rattled the ice in my gin, then drank. "Are we done?"

"Not even close." Safia shoved her hands into her jacket pockets, frowning at me. "Peaseblossom's a PI, one of the guys I hired after you quit. He found a lead and he needs your help to chase it down."

"Right." I stared at her. "No chance in hell. Are we done?"

"I have 'til the end of your drink, remember?"

I took another long slug, left nothing in the glass but residue and melting ice. "I changed my mind."

The hand on my arm clamped down, keeping me seated. "Just listen, okay?"

"No. I've heard this story, Saf. You've thrown money at every con man who's tried it on since your sister vanished, and it's gotten you nowhere." I shook myself free of her grip. "I mean, let me guess: Peaseblossom contacted you, said he had some clue about where your sister is and promised you all kinds of results if you gave him money. I mean, Harry Peaseblossom? Fifty bucks says that's a fake name."

Safia's face went stony. "So."

"I told you to trust investigators Walt found for you. They'd be the most likely to help."

She folded her arms, drawing up straight in her chair. "Like you, you mean?"

I shook my head, weary. "Yeah, fine, like me."

"You realise you quit, right? Like, six times now."

We stared at each other. The hubbub of the bar filled the empty space in our conversation.

"Fine," I said. "So where did Mister Peaseblossom come from?"

"He contacted me." Safia relaxed a little, toying with her glass of Coke. "About three weeks back. Dropped me a card, arranged a meeting, said he'd heard about the reward for information and done some research in his own time."

"Fake name and a miracle lead," I said. "Very fucking convenient."

"To be honest, I don't really care," Safia said. Anger seeped into her voice, cold and sharp. "I've trusted worse, in the past. As long as he gets my sister back, I'm okay with it."

"It's been seven years, Safia. Seven years and no clues, no leads, no fucking sign of what happened. Consider that a good reason to save your money for a therapist and move the fuck on."

Safia fidgeted with something in her jacket pocket. "He did find a lead, Miriam. A solid one."

I pulled the soft-pack of Camels out of my jacket pocket, tapping the last one free. "You want to place a bet on that?"

"If that's what it takes."

"It's not," I said.

Safia slipped something out of her pocket, sliding it along the hardwood bar. It was a credit card, the design a few years out of date, with Uma Mulani's name spelled out in raised letters. It'd seen better days, all caked with dirt and faded, but the details were still good enough to make it seem authentic. Maybe it was, but after seven years with no news I didn't trust a big break in any case. I sure as hell didn't trust one on a case I wasn't working.

"This guy, Peaseblossom, found this?"

"Dropped it in my mailbox yesterday," Safia said. "He says he needs your help to find out more."

I rolled my unlit cigarette between two fingers. "Why me?"

"I don't know," Safia said. "Something about this being in your field and you knowing the case. He said you'd worked together, long ago. He wants a meeting tomorrow."

"And if I can't be hired?"

"Then I'm screwed." Safia leant back against the bar, rubbing at the side of her face. "I don't know this guy, Miriam. I get that and I'm sorry it pisses you off, but he's working my case and you walked away from it. So what if he's lying about his name? He's tracked down Uma's credit card and he says he can do more, and if you're the damn price of doing that then I'm swallowing my pride and asking you to help."

She took a deep breath, waiting. I picked up my empty glass and considered the thin seam of melted ice in the bottom. "I'm not doing this cheap," I said. "Especially not for shit like this. Clues don't show up seven years after they're useful, I don't know anyone who uses the name Peaseblossom, and the people I used to work with either hate me or deserve to be shot. The whole damn thing stinks, Safia, and I'm not going to be shy about saying it."

"But you'll do it?" She reached out to reclaim the credit card.

I closed my eyes. The headache lurking behind my right eye bloomed into a dull, steady pain. "Fine," I said. "Just tell me where and when."

The meeting was scheduled for the Tennyson Point Café. That was the first bad sign.

The Tennyson sat alongside the city gardens, discretely tucked behind a row of threadbare pines. Its red brick walls and wide verandah are associated with the other heritage-listed buildings dotted around the city, but its historical value was up for debate. A row of lanterns hung along the outside of the café, candles glimmering behind the glass. Pine needles danced across the bitumen, carried by the cold wind. I let Safia get out of the car before checking the Beretta holstered beneath my jacket. On the whole, I should have let her worry. The Tennyson was a faerie joint, one of the places the exiles hung out when they didn't want to worry about picking up a stainless steel knife.

Safia didn't believe in faeries. That'd been part of the problem back when I first took her case. I didn't have that luxury. I still had the scars to remind me why messing with the fey was a bad idea.

The cool wind followed us through the front door, drawing attention from the patrons close by. The humans glanced at us and went back to their meals; the fey stared, and the number of mismatched gazes among the crowd made me nervous. Back when I worked homicide the fact that I'd been tight with the Faerie Queen was pretty well known among the exiles trapped in town, and my notoriety had only grown since Anya Titan and I had parted ways. I'd place good money on the fact that half the fey in the Tennyson were thinking about killing me, and the rest were coming up with something snide about the fact I had Safia at my side.

I tried to shrug it off as we ordered drinks. A short black for me and a Diet Coke for her, both on Safia's dollar. The waiter all but leered at us as he wrote the order down.

Safia settled into her seat. "They know you here," she said, glancing around the room. "It doesn't seem like your kind of place."

It wasn't. Never had been, not even in the old days. The interior of Tennyson Point sported mismatched frescoes along the walls, impressionist renderings of ancient, towering forests you'd have to drive a good three hundred clicks to find anywhere near town. It served hamburgers that didn't really deserve the name, artful constructs of meat patty and sweet potato and mango relish that you couldn't eat with your hands. For all its veneer of respectability, Tennysons Point's rep said it liked to keep things quiet.

I felt him coming before I saw him. That was the second bad sign.

It started with pressure behind my eyeball, then a faint tugging on my eyelid every time I blinked. Muscles bunched, alert, and the lingering pain in my chest and shoulder reminded me why I'd accepted Queen Anya's Vengeance in the first place. It felt like a kiss, like the barest hint of tongue pressed against the eyelid, drawing my attention towards the entrance. I gave in and Barry Gideon stepped through, bustling forward until the door closed behind him.

I took a few ragged breathes, trying to stave off the rush of panic, as the blood drained from my face.

Safia put her hand across my forearm. "You alright?"

The cool winter air burned against my skin. "Fine," I said, nodding towards the door. "That him?"

Safia looked. "It's him."

"Damn."

His name was Barry Gideon and the Queen of Faerie wanted him dead. I knew this because I'd been the idiot who agreed to do the job, then walked away from it because I wasn't built for murder. He'd grown older and fatter since the last time I'd seen him. The mohawk remained and the tattoos had grown thicker and the little bit of faerie Vengeance that lived inside me howled for his blood with renewed vigour. Gideon hovered by the counter, watching my face. He took a cautious step forward, gauging my reaction. I pulled my fingers into tight fists to keep them from moving. "Safia?"

"Yeah?"

"There's a gun holstered on my right shoulder," I said, my eyes never leaving Gideon's face. "Take it and hide it. I'll shoot him if you don't."

Safia reached out, her hand hovering by the collar of my coat. "You're kidding, right?"

I gritted my teeth. "I'm really not."

She slipped the gun free and it disappeared beneath the table, a white napkin folded over it. Gideon grinned and waved. He was forty-three and still dressing like a teenager, getting about in blue jeans and the same battered army jacket he'd always worn. There was something awkward about him while stationary, like he hadn't grown into the wide ears and Coke-bottle glasses, but all that dropped away as he loped towards the table. He'd lost some teeth to beatings over the years, at least one of them mine the last time we'd met up. The new gaps in his smile suggested he hadn't lost many of his bad habits.

I guess, in a way, neither had I. All I really wanted to do was work Gideon's smile over with a tyre iron.

"Miriam Aster," he said, "fancy seeing you here."

It didn't help that he didn't sound surprised. I curled my fingers around the coffee cup, keeping myself distracted, then put it down when I considered jamming it against his face and slicing his forehead with the shards. "Walk away, Gideon." My voice stayed low and steady, a last ditch attempt at calm. "Sitting there's stupid and you know it. Just walk away, now, and keep on walking."

"Sorry, Aster, that's not going to happen." Surviving the opening exchange seemed to give him confidence. Gideon sat, hooking an arm over the backrest. I counted six ways I could hurt him, all of them easy now he'd relaxed his guard. "You, me and Miss Mulani need to talk about her case. Put your palms on the table and breathe deep, Miriam, 'cause I need to be here for a little while."

I did as he said, fingers spread wide. Gideon leaned over towards Safia and offered her his hand. "Peaseblossom," he said, "a pleasure to meet you face to face."

Safia opened her mouth to respond but I cut her off. This time the words hissed out through clenched teeth, my control slipping away. "What do you want, Gideon?"

Gideon hovered, hand outstretched. When Safia didn't take it he folded the stubby fingers across his stomach, offering us both a bland smile. "You'll have to excuse Aster's manners for the next couple of minutes," he said. "She's trying very hard not to kill me right now."

My index finger tapped the tabletop. "Maybe I'm trying too hard, Gid."

We stared at each other. Safia cleared her throat. "Miriam?"

"His real name's Gideon," I said. "He's a killer."

Safia raised an eyebrow. "Yeah? Who'd he kill?"

I took a slow breath. "Me."

Safia looked at me, waiting for some sign I was kidding. I didn't give her one. It's hard to joke about dying once you've rolled through the experience once or twice, and I had the morgue scars on my chest to remind me how unpleasant the whole ordeal had been.

Gideon's grin showed off his teeth. "So we're going there, then." He shook his head with mock disappointment. "You're not still holding a grudge about the deal with the unicorn?"

"There was another one loose recently," I said. "It reminded me of the bad old days."

"You should learn to let go of the past, Miriam. After all, it's not like Her Majesty let you stay dead."

"Shut up."

"Still, it might have been a mercy if she had." Gideon cocked his head. "I've heard rumours about how much you're drinking these days. It can't be healthy."

"Shut up and get out," I said, "unless you've got a real good reason why I won't be spending the next hour kicking the shit out of you."

"I've got two, actually." Gideon held up two fingers, then folded one down. "First, I really can track down her sister if you help me. She's been kidnapped by faeries, Aster. I can't force them into giving her back but you can."

My hands trembled against the tabletop, eager to be moving. "No-one's been kidnapped by faeries in ten years Gid. The gates to Faerie are closed."

"There are still ways, and you know it" he said. "Back paths and secret gates, the faerie rings out in the forest on a full moon. The Lords of Faerie aren't game to cut us off completely; the paths that remain are dangerous and unpredictable and only idiots try to walk them, but they'd do the job if someone was determined and there's no-one watching the mortals' backs anymore."

I leant forward, my voice low. "You're saying this is my fault, Gid? That I should have stuck around and kept doing my job?"

"I'm saying it's been seven years since Miss Mulani's sister vanished," I could smell the harsh scent of Gideon's lingering fear, sharp and metallic beneath the salty sweat. His presence pressed against my skull like a weight, his pulse like a steady drum against my ears. "Seven years, Aster. Seven years missing and not a single Goddamn clue; did it really never occur to you that she'd been kidnapped by our old friends?"

I let my breath out slowly, reigning in the anger. "It did, but it wasn't likely. She was an adult, she'd be noticed. Neither of these things are prime targets for an abduction."

"And yet I had the credit card." Gideon tilted his head towards Safia and gave me a nervous grin. "Tell her you think I'm lying, if that's what your gut says."

He waited. I stared at him. The fey in the café were watching again, a dozen pairs of mismatched eyes glimmering in the candlelight.

"Fine," I said. "What's the second reason?"

"I'm being chased by a bogeyman." He wilted, the confidence leaked out of him. "A really bad one, dangerous as fuck. And if you don't help me get rid of the bastard, it'll be more than Miss Mulani's sister that suffers."

He said it too loud, attracted more attention than we wanted. I pitched my voice low, trying to get him to calm down. "There's no such thing as bogeymen, Gid."

"You'd know that better than I." He stood, keeping his hands in plain sight. "I handled the exchanges between civilized fey, Aster. I might not know this thing's species, but I know I have the problem and you're the best shot I've got of staying alive. Take care of whatever this is and you'll get Miss Mulani's sister back."

A shadow fell across the table, the waiter stepping between us and the light. The waiter's eyes were two shades of green, like the subtle differences between a real emerald and something made in a lab. What little amusement the fey had seen in gossiping about my presence was gone. "You're disturbing the other customers," he said, directing the comment to the back of Gideon's head. "We'd like you to leave now, sir."

Gideon looked up, a sudden streak of panic running through his voice like a riptide. "Come on, buddy, just give me a moment."

"Sir," the waiter said. The rough snarl of his voice was enough to put a chill through my intestines.

"Jesus." Gideon's voice took on a wheedling note. "I just need—"

The waiter put a hand on Gideon's shoulder. Not hard, not insistent, but it was enough. Gideon stopped, looking up the arm, searching the fey face. It wouldn't be much of a fight, if Gideon chose to make it one. The faerie started escorting him towards the door.

Safia turned to me, her eyes narrowed. "That's it? You're just going to let him walk?"

I thought about it for a second. It would have been easier if I hadn't.

"Wait," I said. The word leaked out through numb lips, seeping through the hole in the dike holding back my anger. There wasn't much give in the order and the waiter froze, hand on Gideon's arm. I looked up, staring at the light reflecting off Gideon's glasses. "I'll need some real proof about her sister before I do anything. A credit card won't cut it with me, they're easy enough to fake and you're dumb enough to try it."

Gideon tilted his head in my direction. "I'm squatting out on Palm Tree Row," he said. "Pretty sure you can guess where. Meet me there in three hours and I'll have all the proof you need"

CHAPTER 2

The mood in the car was icy as Safia drove me home. Rain hammered the city like the clouds were holding a grudge and I sat in her passenger seat, hands twisting into tight fists, fighting the sharp jags of anger running through me. Safia's tape-deck stayed quiet, leaving us with nothing but the hiss of wet tyre on the road. Deep breaths didn't help. I flicked the stereo on. That didn't help either. I wasn't sure why Safia was pissed and I didn't much care. There were two possible conversations that could follow our meeting with Gideon, one full of lies and the other full of dangerous truths. Neither possibility excited me. Then Safia took the decision out of my hands.

"I know he's not crazy," she said, taking her eyes off the road to make sure I'd heard her. "I know there are faeries, Miriam. I know they could have kidnapped my sister. Don't try and play it like he was crazy and use that as an excuse to walk."

My hands stilled, knuckles digging against my thighs. It should have been good news, but all I could see was the potential trouble. There wasn't much question about who'd been the one to tell her. "Bloody Colton. Stupid bastard can't leave well enough alone."

Safia didn't answer, just turned the stereo down and kept driving. I listened to the rumble of thunder and the soft tap of rain against the roof of the car. A pop song whispered through the car speakers she hadn't quite switched off. We made it halfway through the song before she spoke. "I asked him about you, right after you quit. He told me stories, a whole bunch of them. I didn't want to believe them, but when Peaseblossom showed up and mentioned his theory…"

I counted to ten. It helped. "Colton's full of stories," I said. "Most of them are crap. Gideon's even worse."

"Walt said you weren't just a cop, Miriam. He said you used to work for some queen, you used to stop things like this happening." There was accusation in Safia's tone, but she was doing her best to hide it. She frowned, picking her words carefully. "He said you were good, the best, before you quit."

My laughter was bitter. I couldn't help it. "Walt's overly generous," I said. "I was a just a sucker. The faeries used me, Saf. They keep people like me around because we're useful, because we keep their existence secret and cover up the occasional murder when one of their kind gets antsy. If we were really good, they'd help us find the killer and send him back to faerie where there weren't any mortals to savage."

"Except the ones they stole. Like my sister."

"Right," I said. "If they stole her."

We stopped at a red light and watched two cars pass through the intersection, blurs of colour against the rain. "You set me up in there."

"I know. I'm sorry." The light turned green and she put the car in gear, focussing on the road to stave off the guilt. "Peaseblossom told me to bring you along if I wanted to see Uma again, and he had the credit card—"

"Yeah? Well, so fucking what? You could have told me that's what you needed." I blinked and I could feel Gideon out there, his existence tugging at me. The fire was back, like it'd never left. Seeing Gideon up close was like blowing on an ember.

"Would you have come?" Safia glanced at me, her head tilting in my direction. "Honestly, if I'd told you?"

I pulled the cigarettes out of my pocket and moved to tap one free. Safia glared at me angrily, one hand leaving the wheel to grab at me. "Not in my car."

My eyes drifted down to her hand on my arm. "I'll wind down the window."

"It's raining," she said.

"And you fucking set me up," I said. It felt good to get irritated at someone else, to feel a little of my own anger fill up the spaces the Vengeance didn't touch. "You don't have much of a high ground."

"Bullshit." Safia hit the indicator, pulling the car over to the curb. "You want to argue right now, Miriam? Fine, let's argue."

The stereo went dead, leaving us with rain and thunder. Condensation on the windows rendered the outside world vague shadows and blurs of light. I tucked the cigarette back into the pack and retreated into formality. "I'm not going to shout at you, Miss Mulani. You aren't paying me to argue."

"Yeah? Well maybe I want to scream at you for a while." She grabbed my cigarettes and threw them into the foot well. "Because, fuck it, yes, it was wrong I didn't tell you, but what other choices did I have? You walked away, remember? I wasn't going to miss a chance to find out what happened just because you weren't comfortable working for me. It's not like I asked you to leave."

"I had too."

"Bullshit."

"You tried to kiss me."

"I did more than try."

"I never asked for—"

"No, but you were there. You didn't seem to mind."

"That just means I'm human." I glanced into the darkness around my feet, trying to spot the lost cigarettes. "Listen, Safia, you were a client, I was fucked up. And I have a history of making bad decisions when things like that happen. It was better for both of us if I walked away."

"Seems like there's more people than just you and me involved in this, Miriam." Safia's hands gripped the steering wheel. She stared at the traffic rushing past in the rain. "After talking to Walt, it seems like you walk away from lots of people."

"Don't even go there. I left you the case notes and the names of good replacements." I leaned forward, my searching fingers latching onto the cigarettes where they'd landed by my toes. "They'd have done the job if you'd let them."

"Maybe, but they weren't friends," she said. "I thought you were."

"Yeah, well, maybe you thought wrong." I opened my door and stepped out into the rain. "I need a damn cigarette. Give me a moment."

The door didn't slam behind me. There wasn't much point in that, given the size of the compact bubble Safia called a car. I scrambled for the bus shelter a few metres away and lit the cigarette with tingling fingers. Rain filled the gutter, pooling where the drain was clogged.

Safia dashed from the car to join me, her jacket hunched over her shoulders. I huddled, smoked, tried not to look at her. "Christ, Safia. I went in there with a gun. You have no idea how close I came to fucking things up."

"Obviously not," she said. "You could have told me about the faeries, you know. If you'd suspected all those years ago, I was okay with knowing."

"Tried that once, started hinting at the possibility." I pulled my jacket tight, held the cigarette out of the wind. "You chose to believe I was joking, remember?"

Safia sank onto the aluminium bench, rubbing at her eyes. "You could have convinced me otherwise."

"It was safer if I didn't." I breathed against the cigarette, savouring the taste. "People who know about the fey tend to get killed."

"I can take care of myself."

"No," I said, "you really can't. Not against them."

A bus pulled up in front of us, its doors hissing open. No-one got off.

Safia scrubbed fingers through her hair in frustration. "I was kinda hoping you'd tell me it was a joke," she said. "That you and Walt and this Gideon shit pulled some elaborate prank."

"I wish." I settled in next to her, kicked the heel of my sneaker against the concrete. ""Gideon used to handle this shit, back in the old days. He monitored who stole children and how to get them back, reported it when things got nasty. If your sister was kidnapped, then he'd be the bastard to know who did it."

Safia watched my face, waiting. "But?"

"But the fey don't kidnap adults and they don't take people who are going to be missed," I said. "They can't risk someone like you hiring someone like me. There's a fifty per cent chance Gideon's running some scam; if he isn't, it's time to start panicking."

"Faeries are that bad?"

I scratched at my chest, at the intersection of the scar tissue I'd picked up after my first autopsy. "They're worse," I said. "So much worse than you're thinking. Faeries are predators, Saf. They feed on belief and love and terror. A few of them exist in our world, trying to be nice about it, but the ones who live in their homeland—" I shook my head, trying to shake off the thought. "It's not good, it's really not."

Safia rolled her heels along the concrete. She frowned, her eyes focussed on the street. "Sounds like Walt left some details out of his stories."

"That's because Walt's smart," I said. "The most involved he ever got was forgetting to file the occasional report when it'd shine a little too much light on the city's fey inhabitants. He never got any deeper and he never wanted to."

"And you?"

"I'm a fucking idiot." I finished my cigarette and flicked it into the gutter. "I do stupid shit like meeting up with Gideon to see if he's got the proof I wanted. If he has then you're still a client, and you owe me a fuckload more than you thought when this job is done."

Palm Tree Row smelt like saltwater and diesel fumes, the legacy of the marina on the far side of the river. The glow of the motel signs gave the row its name, their images and names a medley of neon palms and bikini girls and perfect island scenes lit up on all sides. The tiny promises of paradise on offer had probably seemed apt fifty years back, but the Row had gone downhill after it got swallowed by the urban sprawl, transformed from a small holiday oasis to a claustrophobic outer suburb pressed against the polluted estuary that marked the northern edge of the city. These days the units got rented out as cheap accommodation, short-term leases with few questions asked, and the hotels attracted the kind of folks who preferred to pay by the hour. Traffic rolled through the Row in sparse bursts, taking the old highway route that'd once been the best way out of town. I drove the Row's length twice, doing a lazy loop. The kids clustered under the Seven-Eleven's awning stared at me as I cruised past, their faces bored and thin beneath the overhead lights.

Me and the Row had a history. Ten years back the first name on Anya Titan's shit-list had holed up in an apartment on the southern end of the street. Back then it'd been the Paradise Palms, all pink pastel and plastic flamingos on the lawn, a cheap slice of home for the terminally tacky. Dugan rented a top floor unit, a little breadbox of a holiday flat that always stank of stale chips from the fish and chip shop next door. He'd adopted a minimalist, messy décor, all half-read books and scribbled notes on the fey, the only furniture in the place left there by previous tenants. The Paradise Palms didn't operate anymore. Someone had fenced the whole thing off and scheduled it for demolition, but the process had stalled a year back and now it just hung there vacant. As far as I was concerned, it couldn't happen to a nicer joint. If Gideon was squatting, he'd pick there. The fey didn't mess with the places where Vengeance was extracted.

I arrived early. Gideon wasn't there yet. I knew it climbing out of the car, his absence a dead spot in my heart, but there was still something lurking in the abandoned husk of Duggy's old home. I got the familiar itch on the back of my neck though, my own personal storm-warning that weird shit was due. I leant into the car and popped open the glove box, pulling free the steel knuckle-dusters I kept there for special occasions.

I'd been waiting nearly half an hour before my phone rang, registering an unknown number. I flipped it open and got rewarded by street noise on the other end, a constant flow of trucks and cars that was far from the sporadic burst of traffic moving through the Row. Gideon's voice cut through the buzz. "You there"

"Yeah, I'm there. Where the fuck are you?"

"Safely distant," he said. "Call it a precaution. I figured you, me, the memories of the past; why tempt fate, you know?"

"I don't want to be here, Gideon. Don't be a smart-arse."

"You don't have much choice, Miriam." He hit my name like a full stop, making a point of irritating me. "Look, I went clean after that shit went down, same as you did. I fucked off to the other side of the country so I wouldn't be in your face. I stayed away from anything with butterfly wings and magic, and I tried to have myself a life. That means anything that's after me, anything this big, is chasing me 'cause of that last deal Duggy made. There were plenty of people unhappy about that one, Aster, not just you and Her Majesty. I figure maybe one of them wants payback and they're using Dugan to track me down."

A cluster of teenagers peeled off from the Seven-Eleven two blocks down and started making their way along the street, their voices hooting into the night air. I pocketed my left hand, looped my fingers through the steel knuckles, and peered at the third floor of the Paradise. "Patience, Gid? Assume I have none. You promised me proof about Uma Mulani."

"I lied," he said. "There's no more proof to get. She's in Faerie, Aster. That means no contact until a full moon or someone on their side reopens the direct gates. Besides, you already believe me, you just don't want to admit it."

"Not good enough," I said.

"It's as good as you're getting." There were nerves in Gideon's voice, a little tremor I could only hear because the Vengeance let me catch it. "And you can't take the risk I'm lying."

I swore at him a few times. Gideon waited it out, let me regain my composure. "I need you to poke around inside," he said. "Just tell me if anyone's messed around in there, if there's anything left behind that'd explain why people are pissed. Get me a who, Aster, and I'm golden. I'll take care of the rest myself."

"It's been years, Gid. The cops searched the entire place pretty thoroughly during the investigation."

"Maybe, but I'm a desperate man." A long, loud moan screeched past him on the other end of the receiver, a bus or a truck moving at high speed. "And I'm a desperate man with the right hand of cards for this game. Just go and check it out, Aster. Maybe you'll find something the cops missed, a hiding place or some shit where Duggy kept his notes. Maybe you'll find the little prick who's sending this thing after me poking about for clues. Hell, maybe there's some kind of voodoo you can do. I don't fucking care, as long as you get me something. I'll call you in a few hours and give you what I've got on the Mulani girl, if you've turned up something useful."

"And if I don't?"

My phone answered the question with the short beeps of the dial tone. I folded it closed and pocketed it. It felt just like old times again, right down to the stupid games and the vague sense of endless rage roiling away in my gut. I studied the building and the chain-link fence. There were lockpicks in my glove box, along with a flashlight and some other gear for when I needed to commit a little B&E, and the graffiti covering the lower floor of the building suggested that the fence wasn't much of an impediment. I fished out the gear and went searching for the gate. I found it hanging loose with a long chain connecting the halves. Easy enough to slip through if you're fifteen and eager, and only slightly tighter if you're older and determined. I took the stairs two at a time, heading up to the apartment Dugan rented the first time around.

The pink paint on the door to Apartment Twelve had seen better days, but the deadbolt looked sturdy. I reached out to test the doorhandle, just in case, and déjà-vu broke over me like a wave. For a moment I flashed back to the first time I'd been here: *twenty-seven and stupid, fresh from the morgue slab with gun in hand. A boot to the door and the hinges went, calling Duggy's name in a sing-song voice, stepping over the threshold, the sutures on my chest aching, pulling taut as I breathed deep, crossing the room, Dugan's sweat in the air, sniffing him like a bloodhound as he scrambled for cover, the way he screamed as the first two bullets hit him, puncturing his stomach, standing over him, gloating, "Gut shot, Duggy, a slow way to die," reaching into my belt and pulling—*

I jerked my hand away, cutting off the sudden rush of memory. I stepped back and stared at the doorknob sitting loose in the socket. The faint smell of carrion hung in the air. Magic, then, it had the stink. I took care not to touch the door as I slid the lockpicks in, cursing my lack of practice as I jimmied the deadbolt open. It took close to three minutes to pop the damn thing, and with the soft glow of streetlights lighting me up from the road and my history with the Paradise, I felt naked and overly visible the entire time.

It wasn't much of an apartment. The front door opened into the grotty kitchen, small and tiled with blue vinyl, an open and empty bar-fridge on the bench and a small pile of laundry sitting in the space where a real fridge should have been. Squatters, I figured. Kicked out when the security guard locked the place down. I pulled a flashlight out of my kit and flicked it on. There were feathers on the floor in the centre of the kitchen, scattered around a blood splatter someone had smudged into a crude sigil I didn't recognise.

I knelt down to check it out, arm-hair still tingling from the magic charge hanging in the air. The blood was fresh, but the symbol was a lure, a way of getting me in. A shadow blocked the light from the doorway behind me, something big and quiet slotting into the empty space like a Goddamn conjurer's trick. Sharp claws ticked against the linoleum, little whispers of movement that hinted at the threat to come.

"You'd be Gideon's bogeyman, then." I stood up and turned around.

It wasn't something I recognised, and that alone bothered me. My eyes slid across it, picking up details rather than latching on: the smooth, yellowing curves of the skull catching a thin sliver of light from outside; the stooped stance and long arms curled against its body, caught somewhere between a bird and an ape, the limbs too thin for the feathery mass of its body; the sheer weight of its presence, terror given form. It pressed against me, latching onto the same impulse for revenge that fired up in Gideon's presence. When it opened its mouth, the incisors grew like the fangs of a vampire in a children's cartoon. The faerie hissed at me.

The teeth were a mistake. There's no such thing as vampires, but plenty of fey mimicked the myth to soak what juice they could out of the lingering stories. Sometimes it came out scary, but most of the time it was laughable.

"You've got to be kidding me," I said.

The faerie crouched, hissed out my name in two syllables. "Ast-ter."

That was probably a bad sign.

The Beretta jumped in my hands, instinct taking over where the conscious mind flailed. I hit the damn thing twice and all it earned me was a bad smell, like the muscle and skin rotted away from the wound rather than it bled. I steadied my aim, took a shot at the creature's skull. The bullet glanced off white bone, chipping a fragment free. The thing straightened its head, a slow creaking laugh emerging from it.

"So, what the fuck are you then?" I holstered the gun and waited, curling my fingers around the comfortable weight of the knuckles. Bullets are little better than spitting when you're fighting the fey. At best they hurt, at worst they piss 'em off, but the kiss of cold steel always gave them something to think about.

The thing crouched, legs coiling beneath it and the skull still staring, the jaw bone flapping loose as it hissed out a single, threatening word: "Vengeance."

The skinny legs uncoiled and the bulky mass pounced.

I fell backwards, swinging wild with the knuckleduster. It made contact and its weight landed against me, thin claws raking at my shoulder and stomach. I went down, bleeding, throwing wild fists at its face. The faerie reeled back from the stainless steel love-tap, screaming like any fey did when you pressed iron against their skin. It made me feel better knowing that. For a moment I let myself think I had a chance of getting the fuck out of there, that panicked flailing and blunt force trauma could carry me through where bullets had not. Then the claws closed around my head, gripping tight, and the impact of my head against the linoleum tile ended any hope of fighting the damn thing off.

The world spun around me, using the skull's empty gaze as a pivot. The faerie's heavy bulk pinned me down; I swung hard, driving the knuckles into its side, the place there should have been ribs. Its skin gave way, bulging like a water balloon that refused to pop. This time its grip wasn't loosened by the iron, and even through the panic I knew I was fucked.

"Go on then," I said. "Get it over with."

The second impact didn't hurt so bad, not after the first. I kissed the floor with the back of my head and the world imploded around me, pulling me down into a long tunnel with the bone face at the end.

I watched the empty eyes withdraw, disappearing into the darkness. I didn't see anything for a long time after that.

CHAPTER 3

When I came to there was someone shining light into my eyes, asking questions about fingers and prodding me in the neck. Voices buzzed into one another in the space beyond the white blur of light. For a moment the world hung there, strange and confusing, then the brain caught a clue and everything made sense. An ambulance crew, a bunch of uniforms, the familiar coppery scent of blood in the air. It read crime scene in every language I knew how to speak, right down to the smell of fresh coffee as people tried to overpower the meaty undertone of eau de corpse. I tried to get up, pushing away the ambos, but someone planted a boot against my chest to push me down again. Their heel ground into my solar plexus, my short coughing fit cut off as the pain began.

I wheezed, struggling to breathe, but I got out Gideon's name.

The answer came from behind the boot. "There's just you and the corpse, Killer. Bad luck for you, I think." The kid behind the boot leaned on me, pushing the weight forward and transferring the pressure from heel to toe. "You've got three seconds," he said. "Breathe."

I sucked in a hungry breath and the heel stomped down again. The kid looked too young to be working homicide, his cheeks ruddy beneath the electric lights the cops hauled in to work by. There was something severe about him despite his pinkish features, a downward angle to his face like the heavy weight of his chubby chin dragged everything else towards it. I rolled a little beneath his shoe, the rough tread grating skin through the fabric of my shirt. It hurt, but it made breathing easier, got his weight against the ribs where it didn't obstruct my breathing. "I don't know you," I said.

"I'm new. Third week on the job." His eyes were a startling blue, the kind of pure colour you only get with contacts. They didn't match the cruel, thick-lipped smile he offered me. "You're something of a legend around our department, Miss Aster. You killed two people with plenty of evidence against you, but things kept going wrong until they threw the case out. Hell, even Internal Affairs struggled to make something stick. The way I hear it, you'd still be working if you hadn't quit, Killer."

"Someone's telling fairytales, kid. They forced me out in the end." I forced a smile across my gritted teeth, disguising the sharp intake of breath. "Prob'ly would have gone anyway, once they started hiring wankers."

The kid shook his head, making a clicking noise with his tongue. "You shouldn't bait me, Killer. I'm not like the old guard. I won't play nice."

I grimaced as he ground the heel in, digging it against my skin. "Point taken."

"You're not useful to me, Aster. You're not an old friend, you're not a convenient name to drop into a case report when things don't add up, and you're certainly not my type." He knelt down and I felt my ribs creak, little webs of pain spreading through my guts. The drop took place in a fluid movement, the foot on my torso keeping him balanced. He wasn't a big guy, but he had heft and balance and it made all the difference. His long jacket spread out across my legs as he landed, the knee pressing close enough to my shoulder to pinch skin. The kid grabbed my face, holding me by the jaw. "The old guard think you're useful, Aster. Me, I think you're shit no-one bothered to flush. The name's Goodman. I've read your file, I know you're guilty, and I'm going to fucking nail you to the wall."

"Yeah?" It hurt to speak, the words coming out in a choked whisper. "You need me breathing for that, arsehole."

"I do at that." He grinned at me, showing off a crooked row of teeth that'd make an orthodontist weep. "For now, anyway."

The weight lifted off my chest and he rose, giving me the space to stand. I tried it too fast, got halfway there before the coughing hit and the lingering throb of pain running through my head convinced me I should eat floor a second time. I staggered rather than fell, lurching sideways until I hit the wall and steadied myself. The room did a couple of rotations on its own, taking a few seconds longer to settle, and Detective Goodman's grim little smile never wavered. The rest of his team ignored us, going about their business. "You're fucked, Aster," Goodman said. He leaned in, standing on his toes to get in my face. He stank of pine-scented cologne and smug self-righteousness. "This time around, there's no way you're slipping through the cracks."

There are rules against hitting police officers, just like there's laws against abusing a suspect. I contemplated the odds of using one to get away with the other, then settled for pulling myself upright and looking down on his forehead. "So you want to let me see the body, kid? Only seems fair if you're going to pin the death on me."

Goodman reared back, a chubby viper ready to strike. "Fuck you—"

"Let her see it." The voice came from the corner of the room, a familiar bark that reined Goodman in mid-curse. Tim Kesey walked over, a cup of cheap convenience store coffee clenched in his fist. He didn't look happy, but Kesey never did. He had the kind of face you earn through a succession of broken noses and long-term exposure to the arsehole end of humanity. He stepped in between me and the rookie, staring down at the younger man. "Back off, Kid. Go help the uniforms take statements from the neighbours."

Goodman glared at me. "You can't cover this one up, Kesey. She was—"

Kesey didn't raise his voice, just dropped into the terse growl that'd frightened rookie cops for three decades. "Go."

Leaning against the wall made it easier to stay upright, soothing the urge to throw up that'd been creeping over me for the last few minutes. I waited until Goodman disappeared through the front door before I let myself sag. "Such a sweet guy," I said. "It's a wonder I ever turned away from your gender, Tim, it really is."

Kesey sipped his coffee, ignoring the sarcasm. "New partner," he said. "Started work three weeks ago. It took them the better part of a decade but they finally pinned me with your replacement."

He tried not to sound bitter. Kesey and I weren't friends, never had been even back when I carried a badge, but we'd been a good team once upon a time and he still blamed me for ruining that. Kesey liked things black and white, and after joining forces with the faeries my career in the Force was anything but.

I offered him a cheerful smile, defence against the coming tirade. "And he's such a charmer," I said. "You should be pleased. They finally found you a shiny new protégé who makes you look nice by comparison."

Kesey grunted into his coffee cup, refusing to smile. "Arsehole or not, he's right. You fucked up big with this one. What are you doing here, Aster?"

"I thought I was here because I killed someone?"

He didn't rise to the bait. Kesey never did. "Don't give me shit, Aster. I've got a team trying to bag-and-tag feathers in the kitchen and someone's done a little finger-painting with blood on the tiles. We've got a stiff, reports of a shot fired, and your shell casing in the apartment. And we've been here before, Aster, you and me. We've been to this fucking apartment and seen the same shit ten years ago. That makes me inclined to follow Goodman's instincts about you, so what the fuck are you doing here?"

"Short version?"

Kesey shook his head, weary as hell. "Do I ever want anything else?"

"I had a case, missing persons. The trail led here, something jumped me, and when I woke up your buddy Goodman decided to do a little dance on my chest."

Kesey's eyes narrowed. "Something?"

"You don't want to know. It went bump in the night."

"Don't they always, when you show up." He finished his coffee and crumpled the styrofoam in his fist. Kesey didn't want to believe in the fey, but he'd been working homicide long enough to know that was a decision you *made* rather than something you assumed without question. Some faeries are vicious bastards with the morality of a pumpkin, and Homicide tended to see the aftermath of their more bloodthirsty impulses. Traditionally, things got covered up and the offenders quietly taken care of, but Kesey was too old-school to let a bastard get away with being a bastard. That made me useful, even after my disgrace. It's probably the only reason he ever forgave me when I slept with his sister in the aftermath.

Kesey pointed towards the bedroom at the rear of the flat. "Let's go look then, before I change my mind."

He pointed to the bedroom doorway, his face grim. I led the way, hobbling a little, the pain in my head a reminder of how hard I'd been beaten down.

There's something unsettling about looking in on a crime scene you've already investigated, especially when you were accused of being the shooter the first time round. The kid lying on the bed was slim and dark-haired, his age and frame a match for the last victim found in the same room. Face down, two wounds on his bare back, the last shot through the head done executioner style to make sure the job stayed done. They'd even dug at his wounds, hunting for slugs, like they're something you've gotta hide after you've left DNA and fingerprints all over the apartment. I did the same thing once, back when I killed Dugan. DNA's the least of your worries when you're shooting cold iron rounds.

I stepped into the room, picking up on a dozen little details my memory had glossed over after the evidence was boxed away in a cold case file. Take away the deterioration the room had suffered while transitioning between flophouse and squat and it could have been Rick Dugan's murder investigation ten years late. The room looked much the same. Small, the white paint going yellow, the floor given over to dirty clothes and small piles of books, the faded curtains depicting a jungle scene with pale pink hibiscus that'd bleached white over the years. There was blood splatter over the wall near the bed, little flecks in an arc right about waist height. The ratty duvet bunched at the base, kicked there during the struggle, the corpse's bare feet tangled in the pile. He'd died slow, despite the gunshot wounds. The first two didn't hit anything vital but the excavation had fixed that once the pliers tore through the exposed muscle to dig the slugs out. One of the uniforms scoured the floor for shell casings, but I knew they wouldn't find any. The perfection of the mimicry freaked me out and it showed on my face.

"Yeah," Kesey said. "That's what I thought."

"Shit," I whispered.

"Squatter, most likely. We still don't have an ID." Kesey flipped open his notebook and read through the details. "Male, Caucasian, approximately twenty-three years of age. Three bullet wounds, professional groupings, chest followed by the head. The first two slowed him down, made him tractable for the torture. The last one finished the job, after a messy kind of conversation. Any of this sound familiar?"

I stepped away from the door, hands trembling a little as I dug for my cigarettes. The pack came up empty and I stared at it with hatred. "It's not familiar, Tim. It's exact."

"What do you mean?"

Dugan's murder was a sore spot between us, one of those that ensured Kesey and I didn't speak much. I picked my words carefully. "Every detail in that room is the same as the first crime scene. Not just the groupings and the wounds, it's exact, right down to the pattern of the blood splatter."

Kesey frowned. "I noticed."

"You can't ignore that, Tim. Get the lab to check the old records. It's a complete fucking copy."

Kesey stared at me, waiting, letting me connect the dots. I glanced over my shoulder, spotted Goodman near the kitchen. He gave me a mocking wave, his smile a little too damn pleased.

"I didn't do it, Tim." I forced myself to stay rigid, refusing to sag or grab at the wall. No point adding evidence to the scene that'd make things worse, even if they were bad already. "I have no idea who the kid is, I promise you."

"Yeah, I know." Kesey still carried the remnants of his coffee cup, stuck with them until he cleared the crime scene. HE stared at the lump in his fist, glaring at it like it held the answers and was unwilling to reveal them. He'd never asked me if I did it, even when the evidence started stacking up. Kesey drilled me about details, trying to pin me down, but he never came out and asked if I'd been the one who pulled the trigger when Rick Dugan died. And hell, maybe I wasn't. The anger of the Faerie Queen is a frightening thing, like a river running through you and all you can do is ride. Sometimes I get to pretend it wasn't me, that it's her rage that pulled the trigger on Dugan and Rasputin alike, but that wouldn't hold up if Kesey started asking.

Lying to myself is easy; lying to a Homicide squad warhorse like Kesey is harder than you think. It wasn't worth calling it a frame up this time. He either believed or he didn't. "Listen, Tim—"

He didn't want to hear it. "We're going to take you in."

"Okay."

His eyelids fluttered and he stepped away from me, focusing his attention on the morgue crew coming through the small apartment kitchen. "This is how it's going to go, Aster. You're going to come to the station, you're going to answer some questions, and then I'm going to do everything I can to get you back on the street. We're going to ignore the feathers and the blood in the kitchen, just a little bit of squatter hoodoo that probably isn't relevant. You're going to stay the hell out of our way until we're done clearing you as a suspect, and then you're going to tell me who to fuck over for bringing this shit up again."

I held my wrists forward, ready for the cuffs. "I said okay, Tim."

"Don't be a pain in the arse, Aster." Kesey closed his eyes, rubbing at the side of his jowls with one hand. "I'm tired of all this. I told you that last time we hired you and it hasn't really changed. Odds are we can pin you for murder and Goodman's going to try, but it doesn't feel right this time. Someone's playing silly buggers and that means I can't catch the bastard. You can, so I'm letting you do your thing. I'll keep Goodman away from you as much as I can, just tell me when there's a dirtbag I can actually arrest and don't make me regret the decision. Are you okay with that?"

I looked towards the bedroom door, the rough array of bad memories hiding on the other side. "Honestly, no. But it's not like there's another option."

"Good." He signalled a pair of uniforms talking with Goodman and his sunglasses. I let them cuff me without a struggle and Kesey watched, frowning. "If I'm wrong about this, Aster. If you were involved—"

"No place on Earth for me to run." The uniform cop grabbed me by the shoulder and started escorting me away. "Trust me, Tim, I know how it goes. This time around, I wouldn't even blame you."

CHAPTER 4

Memories are funny things. I'd spent years trying to eliminate a whole bunch of them, and they clung on persistently despite the application of gin and the day-to-day distractions of poverty. I still remember the first time Kesey locked me away as a murder suspect. A cold night, caught without a jacket, my shirt stained with a narrow Y of my own blood after my exertions tore the hasty sutures holding my chest together post-autopsy. I was guilty that time, two men dead and a third beaten to hell, but I didn't remember much of it. Just the guilt and the self-loathing. The headache that never left.

There'd always been faeries living amongst humans. They congregated in the city after their Queen settled down here, setting up shop as an academic named Anya Titan and working to keep the faerie presence a secret. It was a job that needed peacekeepers, mortals willing to walk the flexible moral boundary that said it was okay to break the rules if the ends justified the means. Walt Colton was one of the first people Anya recruited, a veteran of the scene by the time the shit went down.

I was one of the last, the bitch who ruined it for everyone by falling in love with Her Majesty. The bitch who got betrayed and died and came back from the dead because of faerie magic.

The Lords back in Faerie had rules about resurrection, so when Anya brought me back they went with the only punishment they had left. They burnt the gates to Faerie and all the fey on Earth got trapped here, exiled and alone; no daytrips home, no care packages, no access to the wellspring that siphoned the belief in magic from our world and served as a source of theirs. Our world got a little bit colder and the exiles learned to live on scraps, eking what belief and affection they could from their one-on-one dealings with mortals.

All this because I killed some people. All this because I'd let myself get suckered into a trap.

Kesey tried to protect me back when they discovered my DNA at the scene. Kesey didn't know about my trip to the morgue and he didn't think I'd done it, not even when blood and hair samples put me at a second crime scene a few hours later.

I tried to protect myself because I thought it wasn't my fault. That didn't last. Very few things in my life did, after that. I'd shot Rick Dugan and by the time Internal Affairs realised they couldn't make a conviction stick, I'd worked out that a bunch of things were ruined forever: my career; my relationship; a whole mess of friendships. The fact that I'd let Gideon walk away meant the Queen's Vengeance would punish me in his stead.

This time I didn't have anyone pulling strings on my behalf, but innocence makes a better defence than flagellating yourself in a fit of guilt. I had an alibi for the time of death, drinking at Colton's bar. Whoever the dead kid was this time, he'd been shot long before I got there.

It should have been good news. I should have been celebrating.

But three hours into my incarceration I realised I couldn't feel Gideon out there. I knew he wasn't dead, could feel it in my gut, but for the first time in ten years the Vengeance that let me track him didn't give me a direction. Gideon had gone to ground, and he'd used magic to keep himself safe.

. . .

It'd stopped raining by the time they cut me loose. Kesey escorted me to the front steps as he worked through the usual warnings: don't leave town; don't lose the receipt for the items impounded as evidence; don't get caught lurking around another crime scene. I didn't bother to listen. We both knew the spiel by heart and we knew I wasn't going to listen.

The night was still cold and wet. The wind whipped through the short street, rattling a Coke can along the gutter. Safia Mulani waited for me at the bottom of the steps, leaning against the aluminium railing with hands stuffed into her pockets. It should have been a surprise to see her but the evening had steamrolled over my capacity to react to the unexpected. I tapped a cigarette free of its pack and stood on the top step, retaining the higher ground. "Weren't you supposed to be waiting for me to call?"

"Yeah, I thought that too." Safia pushed herself upright and started pacing across the bottom step. "Then I get this phone call from a guy named Kesey instead, and he apologises for dragging me out of bed but he's got to confirm some information he's been given by a suspect. Lucky for him I was waiting up for a phone call anyway but it's something of a surprise to hear my private detective got detained for questioning."

"Ah." I lit the cigarette, cupping my hands around the warm spark of flame from my lighter. "Kesey's classy like that. Didn't mean you had to come down."

Safia shrugged and leant back against the balustrade. "You want to tell me what they're charging you with?"

"Nothing yet." I exhaled a small plume of smoke into the air. "But they're putting some thought into making a murder charge stick. Seems Gideon wasn't fucking around when he said he was in trouble."

Safia raised an eyebrow. "Murder?"

"Occupational hazard," I said. "People turn up dead and I have bad timing."

"And your friend Gideon?"

I rolled my neck, stretching it out. "Either he set me up or I stumbled into a trap meant for him. One of the two. Didn't come up with the proof I wanted but..."

I let that hang out there, not willing to follow the thought any further. Safia rocked as she processed the news, focusing her attention on the dim light-box with POLICE written in blue stencil. Her face was neutral, her lips drawn into a thin line, and she left her hands trapped in her pockets. "Right," she said. "Fuck."

"It's not that bad."

"It sounds bad."

I shrugged. There was a limit to how much hope I was willing to give her, especially given how long Uma Mulani had been missing. If we recovered her from the fey after seven years, few of the possible endings were happy ones. I finished my cigarette and flicked the butt into the gutter. "Come on," I said. "I need a ride."

It caught her by surprise. She stood there, puzzled, until I turned and explained. "They impounded my car as evidence," I said, "and I'm not in a position to hire one until you pay me."

She opened her mouth to argue. I started walking to cut off her objections. "Come on, before I change my mind. If I can't make you stay at home, you might as well be useful."

Safia fell in beside me, trying not to smile. "So where we going?"

"My place first," I said, "then we're going to meet someone you probably shouldn't. I need some answers and he's the only one left I can trust to give them to me straight."

Walt lived out in Sternwood, one of those old inner-city suburbs that'd been taken over by young professionals when the elderly long-term residents started dying off one by one. On the surface all the buildings were the same: small wooden boxes with corrugated roofing and east-facing decks, all of them raised on hardwood stumps to keep them safe from white ants. In practice the places occupied by the new breed of owner stood out, the renovations claiming the suburb block by block, refurbishing the older buildings in the name of cappuccinos and three-piece-suits and mortgage loans worth more than the original owners earned in their lifetime. I spent the drive noting the preponderance of poorly chosen colour schemes and manicured lawns; the shabby homes of the old Sternwood I used to know were like rotten teeth waiting to be pulled. I pointed directions, saying little, guiding Safia to the end of a cul-de-sac before we parked. I crumpled the Post-it where I'd scribbled the address, slid the revolver from my flat in the holster beneath my jacket. It was a big gun, nowhere near as subtle as the Beretta the cops confiscated. The weight of it ruined the fit of my jacket, made me walk a little funny if you knew what you were looking for. Safia peered through the darkness, studying the front gate.

"I'm not supposed to meet with Walt?" she said. "It's a bit late for that, isn't it?"

I opened the car door. "He's got a houseguest," I said. "A friend from the old days."

Colton's house was one of the renovated masses, but he kept it to the original colours and style rather than painting the wooden slats an ungodly trendy shade like mulled wine or eggplant. The only addition came in the form of a shed, a big double-door job that served as the garage. An automatic light came on as we climbed the wide stairs, our movements setting off the neighbour's dog as it twigged to our presence. Safia twitched at the noise. I'd had the nerves beaten out of me over the years. I hammered on the front frame, kept it up until I heard someone moving inside. Walt appeared a few seconds later, the top buttons of his suit undone and the cravat hooked over an arm of the hatstand by the door. He wasn't one for dressing down, not even at home. Part of me wondered if he'd just replaced the uniform with a suit after he quit the Force. "Gideon's back," I said.

Walt looked grim. "Gideon? Really?"

"You really think I'm going to mistake him for someone else?" I pushed past him, dragging Safia behind me. Walt closed the door and latched it, working his way through the deadbolts and locks. His house was designed to catch the breeze, every room branching off from the central hall. I hadn't been here in over a decade. It seemed strange to be standing there, staring at the line of photographs lined up on top of the fireplace in his lounge room. "Where's the cat?"

Walt waved a hand towards the far end of the hall. "He'll be hiding, given the racket you made. He's been skittish the last few weeks."

"Anything behind it?"

Walt shrugged. "I figured it's just a cat thing, yeah?"

I checked the holster beneath my jacket and Walt frowned at my revolver, familiar enough with the weapon to know what it meant. The gun was old enough to be sold as a fucking antique, a solid hunk of metal operating on simple physics. I kept it around for fey trouble, trusting in its simplicity to keep it working around faerie magic. The slugs were iron, specially made and imported from a different state so they were harder to track.

Walt put a restraining hand on my shoulder. "He's gonna panic if you wave that at him, love."

I grinned. "That's kinda the point."

"I've got to live with the urine smell."

"Fine. Give me your piece."

"Where's your spare?"

"Didn't bring one."

"Rule three of dealing with the fey, love. You know better than to bring only one gun." Walt produced a .32 automatic, pressing it into my hands. "Don't make a mess," he said. "I don't want anything to clean after you're done in there."

I checked the clip and found lead slugs, adjusted the safety before tucking it into the waistband of my jeans. "He still think you don't know what he is beneath the fur?"

"Nah, he let something slip a few years back. Didn't seem much point hiding after that." Walt scratched a thumbnail across his chin as he considered things. "I never had the rep you did, Aster. Not even when I still had a badge."

"So he doesn't know I asked you to take him in?"

Walt smiled, shaking his head. "Nah, love. I kept that quiet"

"That's something, at least." I looked down the hall, towards the empty doorway leading into Walt's back room. "You're still a bastard for getting me mixed up in this."

Walt shrugged that off, turning his attention to Safia. "Aster tell you what you're getting into?"

Safia opened her mouth but I cut her off. "I told her, she just doesn't believe me."

Walt glanced at me, frowning. "You really want to take her in."

I let the question drift past, ignoring Safia's irritated look. "It's her call. I've already told her it's a bad idea, but if the faeries really have her sister it's better we get her used to them now."

"You just said it's a cat." Safia's voice dropped into a deep, angry register. "Unless you've got a lion chained back there, I think I'm okay."

Walt ignored her, tapped the side of his head. "You know I can't let him stay here for long, once you go in there? I'm retired, Aster. I stay the hell out of faerie politics these days. I told you to do the same. Once you compel him to give answers, people are going to notice."

"Maybe I won't have too."

"Maybe pigs will fly without the assistance of a glamour."

"Gideon's up to something," I said. "He's being chased by a faerie I don't actually recognise and he's giving Anya's magic the slip. There's no choice on this one, Walter. I need the cat. Short of going to Her Majesty cap in hand, he's the only faerie in the city who'll give me a straight answer."

"You know I'm going to tell you this is a bad idea." Walt managed a bland, uneasy grin. "I don't really want another excuse to say I told you so, Aster."

"I don't exactly want to give you one," I said. "Go to bed if you want, Walter. Stay out of it. I'll try to keep it quiet."

It earned me a gruff snort as he headed for the lit bedroom just off the hall. "Even money says you kill each other in the first ten minutes," he said. "Straight down the hall, last door on the right. He's still skittish, love. Panics when there's company he doesn't recognise."

He closed the door behind him, leaving Safia and me standing under the soft light cast by the hanging hall globe. Safia grabbed my arm, turning me towards her. "We're here to see a cat?"

"It's not really a cat," I said.

"What is it, then?"

"Sleazy, most of the time, but charming with it. Walt's the only guy I knew who'd put up with the damn thing."

She frowned at me, her fingers clenching my elbow tight enough to hurt.

"Fine," I said. "He's a survivor from the old days. I killed him, he didn't die. A faerie with a decent grasp of magic can do shit like that, weave together little miracles just because there are idiots who believe in things like reincarnation and cats having nine lives. I had Walt pick him up from the pound about ten years ago and keep him safe. We used to be friends, before things went south, and I owed him a favour."

I headed for the back room, flicking the light on as I walked in. Safia brought up the rear, giving me some space. I figured she was giving real consideration to the fact that I just might be crazy, that maybe I was networked into a vast web of crazy bastards who really believed this shit happened all the time. The back room was one of those long, thin spots that old houses accumulated, full of bookcases and knick-knacks and other random junk. It sported the faintly burnt odour of old cat urine soaked into the carpet.

There was a lot of height in that room, plenty of places for something the size of a cat to hide. Safia got halfway through asking me what was going on when the cat jumped me, leaping off the top of a bookshelf with its fore-claws splayed wide.

Getting ambushed twice in the same night is good for you, sometimes. It makes you learn from experience. This time I got my hands up a decent fight of it.

CHAPTER 5

I slammed the cat against the wall, my left hand wrapped tight around his throat while my right fumbled for the .32 at my waist. He was a big Russian Blue, husky and grey-furred. He scratched at my arm with everything he had, searching for purchase. I tightened my grip on his throat in response, putting my weight behind the hold. My jacket gave me some protection from the forelegs, but the hind legs hurt like hell. One raking claw got traction against my wrist, just north of the jacket's cuff, and I gritted my teeth as the cat ripped hard along the skin and drew blood. I squeezed his throat until the hissing choked off. He twisted, shifting his weight, and I jerked sideways with him, keeping my balance steady. Finally I got him pinned long enough to level Walt's gun at the cat's face. "Chill Oscar, or it's gonna get messy."

The struggling stopped. I slackened my grip, letting the cat breathe again. He stayed latched onto my arm, claws hooked on my sleeve, his body twisted around my hand like he was part snake. The low, moaning snarl came from the back of his throat, his skin vibrating against my palm. He glared at me, his eyes two different shades of green and pupils narrowed to angry slits. A thin seam of blood welled up from the cuts inside my sleeve, stinging as the air hit them and a few small drops dripped past my jacket cuff and pattered, gently, against the carpet. The cat dug at my sleeve, searching for skin. I rapped the gun barrel against his skull. "Hey, none of that." It earned me a heavy glare. Like I cared. "Here's how it's going to go. I'm going to ask you questions and you're going to answer them. You fuck with me and I'll put a bullet in your head, got it?"

"Ten years and you're still a bitch," the cat said. "Fuck you, Miriam."

"Wrong answer." I pivoted my weight and rammed him against the wall again, my grip still firm around his throat. "And you don't get to call me Miriam, cat. Not anymore. You and I aren't friends, get it?"

"Um, Aster?" Safia took a short half step into the room, her attention locked onto the cat.

"It's not a cat, remember?" I tilted my shoulder a little, forced the cat to look in her direction. "Safia, meet Oscar Rasputin. He's a faerie, kind of, and he's not normally this pissy. He's just holding a pointless grudge."

The cat made a strangled noise. "Me?"

"You killed me before I killed you."

"I was much nicer about it." He wriggled, trying to create some breathing room. "And you got to come back with opposable thumbs. I don't see what you're bitching about."

"You really want to have that argument? You think it's going to end well?" I tapped him across the skull with the gun barrel again. "I'm here for some information, a few simple questions, and I don't really have the time to play who killed who better. Chill out, okay?"

There's something vaguely disturbing about watching a cat's mouth twist into a grin. "Make me."

For a moment I thought he was playing tough, working under the suspicion he could hold his own. Then I saw the gleam in his eyes, the eager look on his face as I recognized what he wanted. I sighed and holstered the pistol. "For fuck's sake, Oscar."

"I'm a man of tradition," the cat said. "If a virgin, pure of heart, wants a favour from my faerie arse then I want her to compel me, just like they used to in the old days."

"Virgin?" Safia arched an eyebrow from her place by the doorway. You can rattle a girl with a talking cat, but some things will cut through the haze of confusion even if you'd rather they didn't.

"It's not how it sounds, trust me." I daubed the fingertips of my free hand against the scratches on my wrist, gritting my teeth against the stinging flash of pain. Oscar stopped clawing me while I worked, grinning when I held up an index finger streaked with blood.

"It works better when you use something a little more lunar," he said.

"This'll do." I raked the bloodied fingertip through his fur, pushing it the wrong way to cause him discomfort. "Virgin's blood, Rasputin, and I bloody well compel you with it. Play nice and answer our fucking questions, okay?"

The world went away for a moment, reduced down to a single burning point of contact between my fingertip and Oscar Rasputin's scalp. I fought against it, falling back on the cold anger I summoned up every time I had to compel something, the little part of myself that still railed against the unfairness of it all, asking "why me" in a savage voice and demanding an answer. I'd tired of it ten years back, all the trade-offs and favours and connections being forged, back when I worked for the Queen.

No-one who worked for her did it out of altruism. I did it for love; Rasputin did it to earn permission to visit Faerie; shits like Dugan and Gideon did it for money or scraps of faerie glamour, fleeting wishes and sparks of magic that never quite matched what the faerie tales promised. Everything in the faerie world was twisted honesty and equal exchanges, the trade of favours and magic and blood.

I used to pretend Anya picked me because I was a cop, or because Walt used to be my partner back when I still worked a beat, or because me and her had a thing going for a few months before I realised she wasn't entirely human. The truth is much simpler: a young Miriam Aster learned she preferred girls to boys early enough to avoid the boy-girl trial run, and the archaic definitions of magic the fey used meant that was enough to qualify as a virgin. I could compel the fey with blood if I needed to, forge a bond they couldn't refuse. I hated doing it every time. Usually the fey weren't too pleased by it either, loathing the forced submission. Oscar knew me though. The fucker knew me damn well, and he wasn't afraid of submitting if it'd piss me off and get him some revenge.

Compelling him tethered us together the same way Vengeance tethered me to Gideon; it let me use Oscar's presence as an anchor to claw my way back into the world.

Sensation started to return, spreading through me from my fingertip until I could see and hear again, picking up the soft tick of a clock on a nearby bookshelf and the squeak of Safia's sneakers against the hardwood floor as the soft tangle of fey magic washed against her. Oscar sheathed his claws and I dropped him, retreating toward the chair in the corner of the room to catch my breath. My right arm ached and the cuts on my wrist left little splotches against the dark weave of my jacket. Oscar landed on his feet, legs spread wide. The brush of magic left his hair standing on end, transforming him into a puffball. I tried to ignore the little tingle in my wrist, the way Oscar's presence tugged at my mind like a minnow snapping at bread.

Over in the doorway, Safia Mulani backed up a step, rubbing the goosebumps on her right arm. "What the hell just happened?"

"Magic," I said. "Kind of."

Her resolve teetered like porcelain on a high shelf, precarious and utterly fragile. She stared at the cat, watching Oscar try to smooth down his fur. "So ... you're a faerie?"

The cat froze mid-lick, throwing a quick glance my way. I waved my hand in Safia's direction. "I said our questions, Oscar. She's included in the deal. Play nice."

Oscar sighed and sank into a seated position, holding his head as regally as he could. "I used to be a faerie," he said. "A half-breed, at least. I was just fey enough to know the laws and use the magic, and just human enough to be denied a passport whenever

I tried to sod off to Faerie. The cat thing's temporary, a little R and R while I cheat death for the second time. It's not dignified, but it works. Nine lives and all that. You can't make life out of nothing, but if people say something often enough you can tap the belief if you're smart."

Safia nodded like she understood, refusing to panic. I clicked my fingers in the cat's direction, motioning him over, and she threw me an irritated look. I was okay with that - irritation held people together better than panic ever did.

Oscar jumped up on the armrest of the sofa and improvised a crude bow. "Your wish is my command, dear lady."

"Don't get fancy."

"You asked me to play nice, Aster."

"Right. Just—" I shook my head, forcing myself to back away from the bait. I closed my eyes and focused on breathing, refusing to meet the cat's gaze. "It's about Gideon, Oscar. I didn't kill him. I let him get away."

Oscar's ears twitched, but that was all. "That must have hurt, " he said. "She was plenty pissed when you died."

"You should know," I said. "Time and distance cut away the worst of the pain but he showed up again last night. Somehow he has managed to elude the Vengeance since then. I think he's out there, but I can't tell where."

"A fancy trick, but not one of mine."

"Bullshit." I flicked the cat across the ear, making sure I had his attention. "You brought him into the faerie world, Oscar. You made him your lover and you taught him about the fey, and I figure you told him where to hide if things went south."

Oscar looked sceptical. I sighed and studied the bookshelf, looking through the shelves of faerie tales Walt accumulated over the years. "It's not me who's after him," I said. "Not this time. He's pissed off something big and powerful, and if he's dead—"

"He isn't." Oscar cocked his head and gave me a sad grin. "He still loves me, you know. Just a little bit, but it's enough. I'd know if that changed or stopped, one way or the other."

I nodded, refusing to look at him. "Fine, he's alive, and that means he'll have gone to ground using the tricks and places you taught him. Whatever's stopping them from finding him is also stopping me."

"It's that important? I thought you'd happily let Gid die after the shit we pulled."

"I found someone to take care of your reincarnated arse. I was pissed at you, Oscar, but I didn't want any of you dead."

"Even so." The cat screwed up its nose, whiskers going stiff. "It's been years. Why do you care now?"

I jerked my chin in Safia's direction. "Her sister's missing," I said. "Gid's claiming he's got information."

"Oh." Oscar butted his head against my shoulder, a friendly sort of nudge. "It's like that, then."

"No," I said. "It's not. Focus, Oscar."

He yawned and shook his head. "I kept a few places, safe houses and such. A few of them were secure enough that he'd go there to hide, and the deeds were taken care of for the better part of a century. He had keys for them, back when we were together. I never got a chance to take them off him. But slipped through the cracks of Anya's Vengeance? That's big, Aster. I couldn't do it."

"It's a start. You got addresses for me?"

"Do a search for Oscar Moscow on local properties. That should turn them up."

I ran my hand over the cat's head, my lips pulling tight at the edges. "Thanks, Oscar. I appreciate it."

"You compelled me, Aster. I'm just doing my part of the deal. What's he got after him?"

I closed my eyes and pictured the white skull face looming over me as my skull jammed against the concrete. "No idea. It's big, lots of feathers, fangs, human skull for a face. Smells like dead meat if you shoot it, but that doesn't exactly slow it down. Knew my name too."

"Oh."

"Oh?"

The whiskers drooped and the cat looked away. "That's not a faerie," Oscar said. "Not when you get right down to it."

I glanced over at the doorway. Safia stood at alert, but her eyes were glazing over with the first signs of panic. Odds are the worst of what we said wasn't even registering; there's a difference between acknowledging faeries are real and finally encountering one.

"How 'bout you tell me what it is, then," I said. "Then you tell me what I need to do to get rid of the bloody thing."

The cat shrank back, easing himself onto the arm of the chair. "There's another half-breed out there, a guy named Danny Mordred. A necromancer, into fear and death as a source of magic. He figured he could earn his way into Faerie if he figured out how to harness their power. He liked his necromancy, wasn't shy about using non-human parts. He used to talk about a thing that sounded like your bogeyman. Always said it was a big deal, one of those once-in-a-life-time jobbies, but I never heard of him pulling it off."

I flipped open a notebook and wrote the details down. "This thing got a name?"

"He called it a Leech," Oscar said. "The teeth may seem like a joke, but they're serving a purpose. This thing's built to drain something other than blood, Aster. It's a giant fucking battery of faerie magic waiting to be used, animated by the soul of the poor bastard's skull he's used when he summoned it."

"Charming," I said. "What's it planning on leeching from Gideon? He's a bastard, but—" I blinked and felt nothing, realised what'd happened.

"Shit," I said. "Motherfucker."

"Yeah," Oscar said. "That's what I figured. It's draining Her Majesty's Vengeance, Aster. It's using your tether to track Gid down." He paused, sniffed. "If that's what it's doing."

"I don't like ifs Oscar, you know that."

"Gideon's small-fry compared to you and Her Majesty," Oscar said. "And the Danny Mordred I knew wasn't prone to messing with mortals. The kid had a grievance against the faeries, took being trapped here a little harder than the rest. Odds are he's hoping you'll finish the job, finalise the Vengeance and give him a chance to siphon it all." He crouched low, ears flat, as if expecting a violent outburst.

"Right," I said, folding my arms. "Fuck. Fuck."

"The good news is that it can't drain what you're not using," Oscar said. "Leave Gideon alone and it'll make do with what it's got."

I glanced over at the doorway, saw Safia's face growing pale. "That's not really an option," I said, pushing my way free of the chair. "Not 'til I'm sure he's bullshitting about her sister."

"If Mordred's involved, he isn't," Oscar said. "Danny worked with faeries on the other side. A lot of the things that got loose in the city were brought through with his help."

"Things like?"

Oscar had the grace to look embarrassed. "*Things*," he said. "The kind you and I stopped. The kind that killed people and got people killed."

Oscar jumped off the chair, scampering away from my feet before I could kick him. I thought about chasing him down, trying to get a straighter answer, decided against it. "Right," I said. "I'll see you, then."

Oscar settled in the corner of the room, ears flat, and waited until I reached the door. "Aster?"

I turned. "Yeah?"

"Be careful with this Mordred guy. He plays people and he's good at it. Don't lose your cool, yeah?"

I leant against the doorway, watching the cat's pathetic expression.

"I'll try not to hurt Gideon," I said. "If that's what you're asking."

"It's not," Oscar said, "but I'd appreciate it anyway."

CHAPTER 6

If I'd been smart I would have taken Walt's car in addition to his gun, driven off and left Safia on his couch to cope with things. I wanted to, but I couldn't. I owed Walt too much, the kind of favours you repaid with donated kidneys, not hysterical stuntwomen who just met their first talking cat, so I left the way I came with Walt's .32 still tucked into my jeans. He wouldn't be happy about relinquishing the gun but he'd understand the need. The third rule about working with fey, less important than the first two: you can never have too many sidearms.

Safia's nerve broke halfway back to my apartment. Fortunately I had the common sense to put her in the passenger seat, jerking my way through the unfamiliar gear shifts as I got her little hatchback on the main road. She'd been taking it well, the fey and the stuff with Gideon, but there were limits and we'd gone a long way past them. She started hyperventilating while we were stopped at a red light, unclipping her seatbelt and dropping forward, putting her head between her knees without being told. I stepped on the gas a little after that, speeding my way towards the shitty apartment block I lived in. All in all we made good time. "Upstairs," I said. "You need a drink."

"I don't drink." Her voice was muffled and a little weak, but she pulled herself together and sat upright again. "And I think I need a shrink more than a glass of wine."

"Yeah, I know the feeling." I got out of the car, eyeing the shadows carefully. I didn't want to buy into Oscar's theory that the entire mess had me at the centre, but it let too many pieces click into place. I pulled the revolver out of its holster, held it tight beneath my jacket. My neighbourhood wasn't fancy, but even the dregs inhabiting my building got nervous when you openly carried firearms.

Safia wobbled as she climbed out of the car, coffee-milk pale and rattled as hell. I put an arm around her shoulder and hustled her up the stairs, fumbling with the keys as I went. "It's okay," I told her, "everyone gets a little weird the first time they see something like that. Just ride it out."

She gave me a weak smile. "You're shit at making people feel better, you know that?"

"Anger's been good to me. Mine, at least." I unlocked the door and led her inside. "After a while you forget how to rely on everything else."

I flicked the light switch, the bare bulb flickering as it warmed up, and pointed Safia down the hall. "Make yourself at home. Let me know if you change your mind about the gin."

Safia nodded, forcing herself to walk normally as she crossed the room. Her voice came out tight and controlled, refusing to give in to fear. "Tea, if you've got it."

There were three deadbolts on my apartment, but I usually settled for using one. This time I locked them all and found myself wishing for a few more. It wouldn't do shit if something really wanted in, not with the thin wooden veneer on my door, but I could rely on the iron grill across the apartment windows to discourage fey visitors from using any other entrance. It wasn't ideal, but it'd kept me alive once or twice before. "I've got coffee and gin," I said. "Neither's very good."

It earned me a tight, pinched smile. "Black, no sugar."

"You'll regret it." I hovered by the small archway leading into my kitchen, a narrow galley set-up dominated by the microwave and cereal boxes. "You want food or something?"

"I'm fine," Safia said. She lowered her head to her knees, kept it there for a few breaths before rising. "I had a panic attack, a little one. Given the circumstances I think I'm entitled."

"Yeah, I guess."

I disappeared into my kitchen, using the coffee as the excuse to retreat and regroup. The first grimy fingers of sunrise were visible through my window. I found myself yawning.

"Aster?" Safia called out from the living room. "Why am I here?"

"Existentially?"

That got a laugh, short and weak. "No."

I walked out of the kitchen. "You should sleep here."

"Oh?"

"Not like that," I said. "You're still a client and there's something about all this, something hinky. Until I can figure out the connection between this Leech and your sister it's safer to keep you around than send you home. I'll make up the bed for you and sleep on the couch."

She nodded, frowning. "Then this really isn't about Uma anymore, is it?"

"It is, I promise." I dropped into the couch, lay my head back against the cushion. "I owe you, Safia. You hired me to find your sister and I fucked up, I walked away when I shouldn't have. If these fuckers have her, then I'm going to get her back."

"It's not like you owed me that much," Safia said, her voice weary and thin. "I paid you to a do a job once. You did what you could when you left."

"That makes you a client, Saf." I peeled off the couch cushion, forced myself to stand. "You pay me, and I follow the case until I find what you're looking for. That's how it works."

The grimy dawn light eclipsed the yellow glow of the light bulb, changing the spread of shadows across my small living room. Safia didn't say anything, just waited for me to talk. I stood and gathered the empty takeaway boxes.

"I'll put sheets on the bed," I said. "If you want to argue about sleeping arrangements, argue later. Neither of us has the energy for it until we get some sleep."

She left the bedroom door open while she slept, the soft

sound of her breathing underscoring the morning traffic. I crashed on the couch, shivering beneath my quilt. It took me a long while to get to sleep. Insomnia's a habit I struggled to relinquish, even in the face of exhaustion. I dozed off around eight o'clock, just as the distant chorus of engines and car horns started to speed up their song.

A sunset the colour of stale blood sank through the branches of the ancient jacaranda in the heart of Marlowe Park. Tiny flowers fell, caught on the warm breeze like purple snow. Rick Dugan leant against the trunk, a half-smoked Lucky Strike dangling from his thin lips, watching me with bruised eyes. "Make one crack about cigarette smoke being a killer and I promise you won't wake up," he said. "Mordred's got plans for you, Aster, but that doesn't mean I'm going to take your shit."

It wasn't a dream, not exactly. I knew enough to recognise the soft touch of someone messing with my REM. Marlowe Park was a bad memory, all the worse for seeing Dugan there. A foul-smelling breeze rolled across the park, dislodging a few purple flowers from the jacaranda's branches. A few of them settled on Dugan's lank hair like snowflakes.

He pulled the pack of cigarettes from the pocket of his jeans and held it out. I took one. "So how'd you get here, Rick?"

"Magic." He waved his fingers in the air, eyes going wide.

"Very specific."

His smile was harder than I remembered, crueller. I could see the faint ghost of his teeth behind the flesh. "You know me. Never needed to know much more than that."

I lit the cigarette and breathed in, gagging on the foul taste of carrion. "Christ, Duggy. These things are shit."

"Yeah, they aren't pleasant." He exhaled a plume of smoke, studying the tip of his cigarette. "But I'm still dead. I take what I can get."

I spat into the damp grass before grinding the barely-touched cigarette beneath my heel. "It's not good to see you, Rick. Just in case you were wondering."

"You wound me, Aster." He shimmered, skinny frame melting into a fluid mass of feather and shadow. My eyes slid across the body, unable to latch on until Dugan's familiar features asserted themselves. He lay across the tangled roots of the jacaranda. "Seems fair, I wounded you around these parts once."

"Fuck off, Rick."

"Not yet." He lit another cigarette, one arm hooked over a looped lump of tree. "There are things you learn about a person when you've got the chance to ferret through their subconscious."

He sagged against the tree roots, mimicking a corpse. I kicked him back to life. "Don't push it, Dugan."

"Now where's the fun in that?" He cupped his entire hand over his mouth when he breathed against the cigarette, hiding the worst of his smile. "Did you know you're not actually sorry about killing me? You tell yourself you are, and you regret shooting Rasputin, but deep down you thought I deserved to die and you're not entirely sorry you got to pull the trigger."

I pushed my hands into my pockets and stared at him, refusing to back down. "If you say so."

"That's the problem, isn't it? It's not me saying so. It's all the things in your head. The little tics you worry about letting loose in case someone uses them against you." Dugan took a few steps forward, his shoulders bulging, breaking out in feathers. The skin peeled away from his face until there was nothing left but skull and the fetid stench of his breath as he loomed over me. "And the bad news is that we're not going to be shy about using those tics. Mordred wants you good and rattled by the time this ends. He wants you ready to panic."

"And you figured you'd warn me for old time's sake?"

Dugan's thin-lipped smile bloomed again, the lips turning translucent. "You're not like most people, Aster. You've seen too damn much."

I stared into the empty eye sockets. "That isn't really an answer Duggy."

"No, it's not." His pale skin melted away, a ruff of dark feathers and shadow pulling across his bare skull like a hood. "I'm not all his, not with Her Majesty's Vengeance as a bond between you and my skull. I owe you, Aster. I want to see you suffer and I want you to know what's coming."

"You've been dead too long," I said. "You're starting to talk like one of the faeries."

"True enough." He used the Leech's laugh. "The truth, Aster: you live your life in a state of terror, you're just scared of the wrong things. You're like a nest of hornets – too dumb to do anything but attack when startled or poked too much. He wants you rattled, I poke you until you're rattled. After you've flared up we get what he needs from the nest you've left unprotected."

"I think we're done with this." I turned and started walking, leaving the jacaranda behind me. The Leech's long, clawed fingers settled on my shoulder, pulling me to a halt. I took a shallow breath, trying not to taste the gut-churning odour. "Fuck off," I said. "We're done here."

I felt the Leech's heavy shape press close to my shoulder, the bone fingers growing tight. "You can't save her," he creaked. "The girl, her sister, you can't save either of them."

I didn't turn, but I lifted the bony claw off my shoulder. "Fuck off."

"You don't love the girl either," the Leech said, it's voice a low rasp.

"Why would I?" I started walking, heading for the concrete path weaving between the riverside pines marking the edge of the parkland. "I don't believe in love. I never did."

"You never had to." The Leech's heavy presence loomed by my ear as he followed, the foul warmth of its breathe against the lobes. "The fey believe in love, Aster, and all the evidence you need that you loved Anya is right there in the fact you're still breathing."

"Maybe," I said, "but there's nothing in that deal that says she needed to love me back."

"And now you become her," the Leech said. "How fitting, Aster. And how sickening."

"We're done, Rick."

"Not even close, Aster," he said. "Not even—"

I woke up. Safia Mulani sat by the couch, coffee mug in hand. "You were talking in your sleep," she said. "It sounded bad."

I blinked a few times, trying to get some focus. "So you made coffee?"

"Bad dreams are one thing. Waking up without a coffee is something else entirely." The couch sagged as Safia sat down, pressing the mug into my hands. "You were right, though. What you keep in your kitchen barely deserves to be called coffee."

I drank. Black, two sugars, the way I took it. It tasted better than it deserved to. "Thanks."

Safia's shoulder jerked, shrugging the thanks away. I pushed myself upright and she sank into the couch, taking the space my boots had occupied and leaning her head aback. "About last night," she said.

I tapped the mug. "Coffee first. Then we argue."

"Shut up." She turned to look at me, head tilted forward and her eyes hard. "I'm tired, you're tired, and if you try to be glib we're going to get loud. Just talk to me Miriam. Tell me what the hell's going on."

"If I knew..."

"You suspect," she said. "That's good enough for the moment."

The mug hovered at a point just below my chin, devoid of the momentum it needed to make it to my mouth. "Yeah, okay. Suspicions I have, but I'm not sure how much I can explain without, you know, crossing a line."

Safia put her hand on my knee. "Then erase the damn line."

I opened my mouth to start, but nothing came out. Safia moved her hand away, the soft pad of her fingertips lingering a few moments longer than the palm. My skin tingled beneath my jeans. I handed her the coffee mug. "Take this," I said. "You'll want something to throw."

"Just talk."

"You were right," I said. "They're after me, but that doesn't mean they're fucking around about your sister. The fey have rules, more than are healthy for any sane person to follow, but they don't lie when they offer you a trade and Gideon knows better than to lie on their behalf. She may not be the woman you remember, if she's been over there this long. Hell, she may not even be alive, but at least they'll give us her body and you'll be able to know."

"I figured something like that." Safia let her breath ease out and blinked against the sunlight filtering in through the blinds. "I'm not trying to be a pain, Miriam, but it's my sister. I just want to know what's going on."

I forced myself to smile. "That's how they get you, the fey," I said. "One little piece of information at a time, one little favour to help out a friend until suddenly you're mired in their world and you're paying the fucking price. The short version: one day I fell in love and she turned out to be the queen of the faeries, a woman named Anya Titan who pulled strings and needed favours and did big things for my life in return. We were together maybe six or seven years and I broke laws the entire time, filed away a bunch of murders as cold cases because the perps were from somewhere else and letting the public know that was bad news for both sides. It wasn't all bad, I made some friends, I had a good woman beside me. Then the friends betrayed me, and the woman I loved brought me back from the dead."

My fingers twitched, curling around a glass that wasn't there, and I glanced over at the half-empty gin bottle on the coffee table. "And after that I did bad things because I agreed to let her put a little piece of her anger in me. I killed Oscar and I killed an arsehole named Dugan, and I'm going to want to kill Gideon for the rest of his natural life. And every day I say no to that, every day I'm not hunting him, it hurts a little more inside my head. That's why there are lines, Saf. It's why I said no to your case after you kissed me, why I would have said no if you'd told me why we were meeting with Gideon last night. Things go wrong when there's fey involved, and you pay a fucking hideous price for it."

Safia nodded slowly, her eyes hooded. "And that's all there is?"

"That, and the fact that I really did die." I pulled up the hem of my shirt, showing off the twin autopsy scars that run across my belly. "Twice now, though one's a little more recent, and I don't think the Queen likes me enough to bring me back if I die a third time."

Safia's hand reached out. They were big, ugly things that ran the length of my torso, the two arms of the Y starting beneath my collar bones and intersecting between my breasts, the skin around them a livid red that still itched all the time. Safia's fingers hovered, close enough to touch. "Can I?"

I let out a breath I didn't realise I was holding and dropped the shirt back down. "Safer if you don't," I said. "I liked you Saf. I liked you a lot, but I've been messed up by falling in love once and when you're playing with the fey then feeling anything gives them an opening. They can leech on that and make you pay for every damn moment you hate them."

"She brought you back from the dead," Safia said. "Maybe she loved you in return."

"She's a faerie and I was useful," I said. "Trust me, all their love is self-involved."

"But—"

Someone rapped their knuckles against my door, hammering hard. I held a finger to Safia's lips and pointed towards the bedroom.

CHAPTER 7

Sunlight did nothing to improve the savage lines on Detective Goodman's face but he seemed less imposing without his boot ground against my breasts. I stood in the doorway, blocking his entry, still yawning and dressed in the same rumpled suit they'd found me in back at the Paradise Palms. Goodman wore a different shade of

black, holding himself stiff as he glared at me with his too-blue contacts.

"You seem to be missing a partner," I said. "Did Kesey get lost on the way here?"

"Kesey's busy." His ruddy cheeks puffed out when he smiled. "Murder investigation, you know how it is."

I shrugged, letting it slide. Goodman waited, just in case I'd missed the jab, sweating a little when he realised a little too late that I wasn't going to fight him. He stepped back, his smile dropping like an opera curtain, eyes narrowing into a squint. I gave him a bland smile, turning my attention to the patchy clouds on the skyline. "You after anything specific, kid, or is this just a social call?"

"I'm not your damn friend, Killer. And don't call me kid."

"You started the name-calling, kid. I'm just keeping up to be polite." I watched the cogs grind behind his stare, weighing up the advantages of taking another shot at me. My right hand slipped off the doorknob, fingers spread against the flat of the door instead. I could shut it hard if I needed too, put my weight behind it. "I've got cases, Goodman, and clients paying me good money to work them. If you want to chat on my doorstep, go talk to station accounting and get them to pay my consulting fee. It's not reasonable in any way, but it'll ensure I don't get bored and slam my door into your face."

Goodman pulled a black notepad out of his pocket and smiled at the last page of scribbled notes, reading through the details before looking my way again. "Do you know a former beat cop named Walter Colton?"

I made a show of considering the question. "Well enough to hit his retirement party when he fucked off to work in real estate. Not well enough that we talk on the phone or I invite him over for dinner."

"So you didn't visit him at four-fifty this morning at his Sternwood home?" The question came out a little snide, the way all rookies ask when they already know the answer. It was a stupid thing to try. I knew better than to play the game and went with the truth instead.

"Me and a client," I said. "We paid him a visit to talk about an old case that applied to the client's situation." Goodman opened his mouth and I cut him off. "The client and the case are both confidential, kid. Accept it and move on. What do you want?"

He studied my doorframe, his chin jutting sideways. "Walt Colton's house was broken into this morning. He resisted the intruders, got beat to hell, and he's been in intensive care for the last five hours. We know you were there, the neighbours heard shouting. None of this looks good for you, Killer, not given everything else that happened last night."

The news pooled around me like spilt water and I refused to soak it in. I left it floating, my face calm, and focussed on Goodman. "That it, kid?"

"I'd like to come in," he said, "you know, just to poke around the apartment and ask you some questions about your visit. See if we can secure any link between you and Colton's attack."

"I'd like to see some authorization, otherwise you can fuck off."

The sharp, vicious smile spread across his features. "Have it your way, Killer."

He hauled off a right hand, telegraphing the entire thing. I stepped back and slammed the door, heard it crack against his knuckles before it rebounded and swung back on its own. He looked bewildered, like he hadn't expected resistance, and it gave me all the opening I needed. My fist caught him against the side of his jaw and knocked him on his arse, the surprise hurting him more than the force of the blow. He rubbed at his cheek, grinning up at me like it made for a good joke. That pissed me off, so I let the tip of my boot catch him in the solar plexus. Breath wuffed out of him in a pleasing rush, his face twisting as he struggled to breathe.

"You're done here, kid." My self control cracked, letting a toxic strain of anger bleed into my voice. "Fuck off, okay? Just fuck off, do your job, and leave me to do mine."

It'd been a long time since I let my anger run hot. It left me shaking.

"Sure thing, Killer." Goodman wheezed a little but his breathing edged towards laughter. "I think I got what I wanted."

He gave me a short salute as I closed the door on him.

I borrowed Safia's car, the slow burn of anger working its way through the conversation as she argued about coming along. A phone call and a friend in city hall ran the deeds to Oscar Moscow's properties, pulling up over a dozen possible safe-houses within the city limits. All of them sat next to parks and reserves, places where old and dormant gates to Faerie were connected to ancient trees or special arrangements of rocks. I worked my way down to the last few places on the list; warehouses, mostly, out in the industrial park. I came up empty three times before I found the right one.

The crisp, cold wind swept down the street as I climbed out of Safia's hatchback, the smell of rust and grease thick in the air. It was a short, quiet street. At the other end of the block a mechanic operated out of one of the oversized sheds. Employees with overalls moved back and forth as the cars migrated towards the workshop. The rest of the street sat silent, the big buildings surrounded by chain-link fences and faded signs that creaked in the wind. There was rain coming, I could smell it. I hit the button to lock Safia's car and made for the gate leading to the warehouse registered under Oscar's name.

It'd been a wrecker's yard once. The husks of three dead cars still sat in the bitumen parking spaces outside. They were older models, boxy. Twenty years out of date, maybe, and old even then. I skirted them and hammered my fist on the big roll-a-door leading into the warehouse itself. The knock rattled, echoing, but it didn't muffle the sound of someone scuttling for cover inside.

"It's Aster," I said, yelling through the metal. "You've got about a minute to open the door before I break in, and I'll be in a much worse mood if I have to put in effort."

I counted to fifty-three before I heard someone moving, heading for the front wall beside the door. It rolled up maybe fifty or sixty centimetres, just far enough for someone to slip underneath, and the beat-up toes of Gideon's Doc Martins stepped into the sliver of sunlight. "Throw your gun through first," he said.

Walt's .32 slid through the dust, skidding to a halt a few paces away from Gideon and the controls for the door. He didn't make a move for it and he didn't ask if I had a spare. It wasn't a smart move. The revolver sat like a comfortable weight in my holster, waiting for use.

"Come in if you're coming in," he said. "I'm not leaving this open all day."

My joints creaked as I lowered and rolled under the door in the dust. My shoulder ached as I pushed upright on the far side. It was a long space, with ledges running down each wall to hold the carcasses of decaying cars. Enough metal to dissuade casual interest from the fey. The dust covering the floor had red streaks, as now did the shoulders of my jacket and the arse of my jeans. Gideon stood by a door mechanism, hand hovering by a big red button. He looked like hell, his eyes pouchy and dark. "You're not dead?"

I brushed off my pants, trying not to sneeze. Focusing on that distracted me from the gnawing hate. "Neither are you," I said. "Not yet, anyway."

The door came down behind me, cutting off the afternoon light. A thin line of glass windows were set high in the walls at the rear of the building. Gideon left a long shadow as he circled towards the gun on the floor.

"Don't bother, Gid." I slipped the revolver out of my pocket, gestured towards the clean space in the middle of the light at the centre of the warehouse where he'd set up a pile of clothes to serve as a bed. "Today's history lesson," I said. "This is the gun I used to kill Dugan. It's the same one I used to gun down Rasputin. Custom made slugs, raw iron in a copper jacket. Think about that carefully, Gideon, because I'm going to start asking questions and I'm really tired of living with a ten year headache because I let you keep walking."

Gideon backed away, eyes darting, trying to figure out an escape route. There were plenty, if he didn't mind getting shot, and I wasn't green enough to stand close to him and give him a chance at the gun. He sagged, his entire body giving up, and he slumped onto his make-shift cot. "Okay," he said. "Fine. Whatever you want."

"Good. So, are you really being chased by that thing?"

"What?" His eyes went wide. "Jesus, Aster. What do you think?"

"I think you've got plenty of reasons to set me up," I said, "assuming you found someone who could actually close the deal."

"You're crazy, Aster. How stupid do you think I am?"

I raised an eyebrow. "You tried it once, remember?"

Gideon's face fell. "We were scared back then, we panicked. Dugan lined up a deal, helped this guy bring some merchandise over from Faerie. There was money in it, maybe even a chance for the homeland if Rasputin did his part right. When things went wrong Dugan said we needed to kill you to keep the Queen from finding out."

"You really thought that'd work? She was my girlfriend, Gid. She'd notice when I didn't come home."

"I thought we could buy time," Gideon said. "I didn't know how much, but Dugan knew people who could help, people who could hide us if she didn't know who did it right away."

"Fine." The gun trembled in my hand, eager to fire. I forced myself to breathe. "So why's that thing chasing you?"

"I don't—"

I pulled back the hammer on the revolver, letting it click into position. Gideon's eyes went wide and he swallowed, searching my face for some sign I was kidding. There wasn't anything there for him, I made sure of it.

"Think carefully about your answer," I said.

"This guy came to see me," he said. "Half-fey, like Oscar, but creepy with it. Said he knew what'd happened way back when, that he could help me out."

"He got a name?"

"Like any of the faeries have a real fucking..." Gideon's eyes went to the gun and he left the thought behind, focusing on the story. "Doesn't matter, I guess. Called himself Danny Mordred. Creepy dude, but he knew his shit. He killed off a few faeries and used their life-force to build that thing, tapped into a whole well of fear to make it live. And he said he's figured out a way to reopen the gates to Faerie, for a little while at least. Said he'd bring Oscar back from the dead if I helped him, that he'd be able to do it, as long as I brought him what he needed."

I took a short step towards him, keeping the gun steady. "Yeah and what was that?"

"You." He looked away, closing his eyes like he expected a bullet. I pulled the revolver away from his face and eased the trigger back.

"That's not exactly a surprise at this point," I said.

He blinked, eyes wide behind the thick glasses. "Jesus, Aster, you could have said."

"I'm not here for me, Gid. You and Mordred can plot all you

want and I don't really care, but if you were going to lie it'd be about that. Now we move on to the bonus question: where did Uma Mulani's credit card come from?"

Gideon's breath puffed out, steaming in the cold winter air. "You're kidding, right?"

"She's the client, you're not." I swung the gun towards him again, the weapon moving in a lazy arc that ended pointing in his direction. "You should know this is the answer I'll shoot you over, if I don't like it. You and me, we aren't important. We fucked up ages ago and our chances of fixing that are long gone. Tell me a story, Gideon. You and Uma Mulani and whoever supposedly kidnapped her. Because if you lied to me about her, if you used some story about her as bait because the opportunity was there, then you and Danny-Fucking-Mordred—"

"We didn't," Gideon said. "I swear to fucking God."

"Then speak," I said. "Fast."

"I organised it," he said, the words rushing over each other in their haste to get out. "Seven year ago, the last time I was in town. I paid some local faeries to get her off the shoot, locked her away at a safe-house until some knights from the Faerie side came over to collect her. It was an in-and-out gig, work for hire. They gave me a list of requirements and she was the one who fit."

I scratched the bottom of my chin with the butt of the revolver. "What requirements?"

"Female, a twin, someone visible." Gideon's Adam's apple bobbed, eyes following the gun barrel. "There were more, but those were the main ones. They were very specific."

"They got names, Gideon?"

"I never asked." He flinched when I lowered the gun at that, eyes squeezed closed. "Come on, Aster, you know what they're like on the other side of the gates, all secrets and riddles and false names. Why waste time asking questions when they're only going to lie?"

"The fey don't lie, Gid."

"You know what I mean, yeah? When was the last time you got a straight answer without offering up your virgin's blood?"

I broke his nose with the butt of the revolver. It wasn't

entirely my idea to lash out, but for once I didn't begrudge the Vengeance for pushing me over the line. "You know better than to mention that, Gideon."

He opened his eyes and glared at me, blood pissing out of his nostrils. "Jesus," he said. "Fucking hell."

"Details," I said. "Convince me. Uma Mulani was known. She had friends and family, she had fans for fuck's sake. Since when do the fey want people like that?"

"What do you want me to say?" His voice rose, edging towards a shriek. "These aren't the old days, Aster, and I didn't ask. Maybe it's changing times, maybe they've got a plan. Either way, I don't fucking know. This was supposed to be my last job, Aster. I wouldn't have even done it after what happened, not if they hadn't promised me…"

"Money?"

"Rasputin," he said, voice low. "They said they'd give me Rasputin back, told me they could find him alive and well. It'd take time, what with the easy ways between here and Faerie closed, but they'd do it. They found a way to collect the girl, and I figured that meant they'd be able to live up to their promise. Then six months ago this Mordred guy shows up, says it's time to collect." Tears welled up behind his glasses, mingling with the blood coating his cheeks and chin as they ran down his face. Gideon edged backwards, watching the gun in my hand. "I swear to God, Aster. I swear to fucking God."

"Then I guess that'll have to do." I slid the gun back into the deep pockets of my jacket and patted Gideon on the head. "Where do I find Mordred then?"

Gideon squeezed his eyes shut again. "You remember that house Rasputin owned? The one out on the farm?"

"Yeah, I remember it."

"Mordred's out there," Gideon said. "I set him up out there, figured it'd be safer, that no-one would go looking. He's hiding, Aster. From you and from the Queen. I don't know what they did with the Mulani girl, but they sure as hell didn't want anyone interfering."

CHAPTER 8

I drove over to the Royal Hospital, watching the storm clouds gather and start spitting angry rain at the earth. The tightly-packed public car park didn't have any vacancies, so I parked on the hill leading down to the emergency vehicles entrance and walked the last couple of hundred metres with the rain stinging my face. When I asked the nurse on duty for details on Walt's condition she gave me an even stare and asked if I was family.

"Sure," I said, "why not?" I don't think she believed me but I managed to grab the ward number when she double-checked the file for the visitor details. Not exactly honest but I do what I can for friends. I hit the elevators and went to the fifth floor, following a red line on the walls to Intensive Care. The hospital made me feel nervous, as though my seedy little life didn't deserve such sterile surroundings. I slipped past the duty nurse on the IC ward and let myself into Walt's room, ignoring the "staff only" signs and the steady beep of the equipment they'd strapped him into.

Walt looked like shit, even by the standards of someone sleeping in a hospital bed. They'd busted the orbital bone around his left eye and done a pretty good job of pulping the eyeball itself. In addition there were plenty of cuts and bruises. Dressings on his chest suggested a knife-wound, or something bigger, maybe even a sword if you were ambitious or the kind of woman who suspected fey involvement. I'd seen plenty of people fucked up by faeries before, mauled by werewolves or raped by unicorns or eaten by one of those swarms of pixies that strip flesh from a living human like a pack of piranha. Those tended to be careless kills, all instinct and aggression. Swords were the domain of the smarter end of the faerie breed. Occasionally they beat the shit out of someone for the hell of it but usually they had a reason.

I put a hand on Walt's shoulder, away from the wounds and equipment. "Sorry, mate," I said. "I think this one's my fault."

"Aster?" His uninjured eye opened, peering through the mess of bruises. His voice was little more than a mumble through the tubes hanging off his lips. "Hey, love, I think I lost your cat."

"Jesus, Walt, go back to sleep."

"Nah, love." He coughed a few times, trying to push himself upright. "Guy who did it ... took the cat."

It took me a few seconds to sort through the mumbling. "Rasputin can look after himself. If I didn't kill him, I can't think of much that can."

Walt's breathing wheezed against the machine. "Tried to stop them," he said. "Got myself stabbed."

"Faerie?"

He tried to nod, but the tubes wouldn't let him. "Glamoured. Pretended to be a cop." He pressed a tongue against his lips, trying to moisten it. "Young."

"Yeah, I figured." I leant over and patted his shoulder. "I'm sorry, Walt. Should never have gotten you involved in this one."

"Thought I got you involved, love," he mumbled. "Take care of Safia. Don't be an idiot about it."

"Maybe you should rest."

"Shut up." Walt coughed again, the sound rattling in his throat. "Shut up and stop blaming yourself. All that shit I told you, back when you first got started..."

"Was right," I said. "Bad things happened. You got stuck with the world's most annoying cat."

"I didn't mind the cat, love. He wasn't bad company."

"Pull the other one."

"Me and him, we're just a coupla old buggers."

"Sure you are." I put a hand on his arm. "Don't die, you bastard, or I'll make you regret it."

Walt didn't have an answer for that, not one he could articulate. His good eye closed and his breathing dropped into a deeper rhythm. I sat there for a long while, listening to him inhale and exhale, just in case it changed. It lasted maybe thirty minutes before a nurse came past and found me.

"Sorry," I said. "Just needed to see him. I owed the old bastard a few favours and it didn't sound like he'd be around much longer to collect."

The nurse shrugged off my excuse and held the door open. "Out," he said, "or I'm calling security."

"I'm going, I promise."

"Out," he said and he stood there watching while I gathered myself, his blue scrubs hanging loose off his scrawny frame.

The rain was falling harder by the time I emerged from the hospital, a cold and steady deluge hammered the ground like a punishment from God. I walked to my car, blinking through the water dribbling into my eyes. My jacket hung cold and heavy by the time I found the hatchback and slumped inside. Taking the cat changed things and not in a way that I liked. There weren't many people who knew Oscar Rasputin survived the three bullets I put in him, and those who did probably didn't know how. He was a smart bastard, always had been, and he'd gotten around more than one attempt on his life.

My phone buzzed in my pocket. I flipped it open, shivering as the wet chill settled in against my skin. It was Safia.

"That cop was waiting for me when I got home," she said, her voice low. "The one from this morning. The one who pissed you off."

My stomach froze, shrinking in on itself. "Yeah? What'd he have to say?"

"Not much."

I fumbled the keys into the ignition, trying to hurry. "That doesn't sound like Goodman," I said. "He's big on the wordplay when he gets a chance."

"He's asking if I hired you to track down my sister," Safia said. "Then he stared for a bit while I answered, trying to get me to back down."

"What'd you tell him?"

"Yes."

I started the car. "Wait, asking? He's still there?"

"In my lounge. I said I was making coffee."

"Hold him there. I'm on my way." I slid the hatchback into gear and pulled out onto the rain-slick street.

It took twenty minutes to hit Safia's townhouse compound and there were cars lining the streets on both sides. None of them had the big, boxy-white look of an unmarked cop car.

The compound was one of those sprawling, walled up blocks with buildings spread around a central ring. A nice place, all whites and blues and pinks, but it set my teeth on edge just to look at it. The blue gate wouldn't stop a determined thief if they really wanted inside. Security sells as a commodity, even if it's just an illusion.

I leaned on Safia's buzzer and got let in.

"He's gone," she said. "Left ten minutes ago."

"Walk me through it," I said. "Your entire conversation with Detective Goodman and the things you said. Let me know if anything went weird while you were talking."

Safia frowned. "You're soaked. At least let me get you a towel first."

"You've got tile floors," I said. "Mop after I'm gone. What the fuck happened, Safia? What did you say, exactly."

She ran me through the conversation again, just as short as the first time around. "You sound concerned," she said after she was done.

"I've never mentioned your sister when I told the cops about the case," I said. "I sure as hell didn't tell Goodman about it."

"So? Uma was known. He might have remembered the news when she disappeared, put two and two together."

"If that's the case he'd be asking more questions," I said. I forced myself to exhale, trying to slow down my pulse. "The guy who stabbed Colton pretended to be a cop and I'm pretty sure it was Goodman, so he's either faerie or working for them. Between that and the cat going missing, things aren't adding up."

"Jesus, Aster. Aren't we out of stuff that worries you yet?"

"Not even a little," I said. "They're up to something big, something ugly, and they're waiting for me to walk into their trap."

"So don't go," Safia said.

I shrugged. "Have to. That's how we'll get your sister back."

"Then take along some back up." She smiled at me, shoulders tense and ready to go.

"Fucking hell, Safia. What part of dangerous don't you get?"

She pointed to the scar across the side of her face. "I took Uma's bumps for four years before she disappeared. I've got no reason to stop now."

I glared but she didn't back away, didn't even flinch as I took a step forward. She could take me if it got physical, I knew that. Stunt work, tai chi, a medley of martial arts training. She was in better shape than me and she knew more about arse kicking, but she wasn't a fighter where it counted. She didn't want to hurt anyone and she wouldn't dream of killing.

"Goodman's playing this strange," I said, "he's the guy who hired Gideon, the one who sent the credit card, he's not exactly shy about using other people to stir the pot. This'll be dangerous, Saf. Dangerous on a whole 'nother level. Mordred's the kind of guy who brings monsters into the world and laughs about it. The faeries who took your sister are likely to be worse. I don't want you used as a pawn."

"Think of like it chess then," Safia said. "Fill me in, get me to the line, and treat the pawn as a queen for the rest of the game."

. . .

The roads were slow in the rain, giving us an hour of taillights and thinning suburbs before we hit the sparse properties just outside the city limits. Trees bordered the road on both sides as we rounded the curve of a small hill, the occasional mailbox marking a driveway that cut through the undergrowth. The old ten-gallon drum nailed to the fencepost of the property had seen better days, the poorly stencilled name already half-lost to encroaching rust. Long grass dominated the slope of the hill, the angled roof of the house just a shadow amid the rain and clusters of overgrown foliage. Short squalls of wind pulled at my jacket as I unlatched the gate. The chains holding it shut were cut, the rusting surface and padlock giving way to grey steel where they'd been sheared in half. The fey didn't bother with it, the Leech didn't need to.

Safia's hatchback whined the entire way up the slope, tyres skidding in the mud as she tried to coax a little more power out of the engine. We got halfway before the car bogged down completely, wheels spinning helplessly in a puddle, and I told her to cut the engine. The interior windows misted over, obscuring the view. I scrubbed a peephole with my sleeve and peered through, getting the lay of the land. The house looked empty and abandoned, the windows shattered and railings were missing from the wide wooden balcony that jutted past the long stilts keeping the house level.

I got out and turned my face to the rain, blinking into the storm. Safia's door slammed shut, and she took a few moments to rummage through the boot, sorting gym bags and work gear until she turned up a long fighting knife in a rubber sheath. She strapped it to her belt, looping it in place with practiced ease. I leaned close to her, shouting through the storm, "You know how to use that?"

"Silat. Five years." She tapped the knife with the palm of her hand, shrugged away my curious look. "Trained for a movie once, kept on going afterwards."

I grunted and started up the slope, letting her follow behind me. My sneakers skidded through the wet grass, sliding straight off wet stones in the old path. Muscles in my legs started complaining almost instantly. By the time we hit the top of the drive I was breathing heavily and cursing the rain. Safia stood beside me, unflustered, and studied the house. The yard had climbed up on it, grass pushing against the short steps on the top side. The door hung ajar, an open invitation, and rain against the tin roof made a racket loud enough to set my teeth on edge. Safia pushed limp hair off her face, her other hand settled on the knife pommel. "At least it'll be dry in there."

"Yeah," I said, "at least."

They'd built the house around a central hall, a straight line through to the living room and a pair of double doors leading onto the balcony. I pulled the gun out of my pocket and eased my way in, securing door by door like they train you in the academy. The place was a mess, bedrooms rummaged by vandals and graffitied throughout. All that remained were old skeletons of furniture, beds and chairs rotted away to wood and spring. My wet footsteps echoed as they squelched against the floorboards, louder and wetter than Safia's light step following me.

We didn't hear anything but rain and thunder and the house was dark enough to justify pulling a flashlight as we moved through. It wasn't until we hit the back rooms that we noticed the house creaking, listing slightly on the unsteady pylons. Safia edged the doors open, looking out onto the covered balcony. There wasn't much there except cigarette butts and dead leaves, which the wind set dancing, blowing them across the greying wood.

"There's nothing here," she said, laughing. "Damn it, Aster, you had me freaked out about this." She turned around, her silhouette framed by the doorway.

I smelt it coming, the dark fetid stink like rotting meat rising up through the creaking floorboards. Safia registered it a few moments later, pulling a face. She turned to me, her nose wrinkling. "Do you smell something off?"

It wasn't the Leech, not quite, but it smelt near enough to make me worried. Faerie magic has its own odour, distinctive as a fingerprint, and even the years of cigarettes couldn't keep me from registering the similarities. I circled, my revolver at arm's length, trying to figure out where it came from.

The smell got stronger as I turned. "Run," I said. "Get out before it starts."

Safia looked at me. "Before what st—"

I never heard the rest.

CHAPTER 9

I was twenty-eight again, the past rising up around me while reality flickered and disappeared like a television signal lost in static. The only thing that remained was the heavy weight of the revolver in my hand. My head hurt, my chest hurt, the rotting scent clung to me like a lover's touch. Twenty-eight again, newly returned to life, and I was getting ready to shoot Oscar Rasputin for his part in getting me killed.

There were little things that struck me, details I never remembered properly that just clicked into place, filling the gap between memory and moment. Everything hit me at once: the way my holster dug into my hip, my gait a little off now the gun wasn't weighing me down on the side; the soft buzz of a Madonna song on the far side of the wall, the volume turned down as Rasputin watched *Rage* on the farmhouse television; his scent in the air, spiced with hints of chilli and cinnamon, sweet and intoxicating as a flower's bouquet. I stood outside his house, gun in hand, and prepared to kick the door down. My lips still tingled with Anya's kiss, her quiet plea before I'd left. "Give me Vengeance," she'd said. "Be my hands where I cannot touch."

Rasputin thought I was dead. I knew that because he was smart enough to run like hell if he knew I was coming. It wouldn't have helped, not really, but it might have kept him to a flesh wound. I could feel him, through the anger, a gnawing presence against my heart and mind. "Miriam?" Safia's voice, very distant, still ten years ahead of me and somehow close. It was a lifeline to the present and shattered the perfection of the memory. I resisted, clinging to the righteous anger, the anticipation of revenge. The way Queen Anya's burning need for revenge wrapped me up and made a lie of the pain, made everything simple and easy and so very tempting. Open the door and kill Oscar Rasputin, sate the need for blood and balance. One girl returns from the autopsy table and her killers go there in return.

I forced myself to breathe, to try and smell the dust of Rasputin's abandoned house instead of the sweet smell of his bong seeping under the front door. The wall felt cold and heavy as I pressed against it, my eyes darted from side to side, but the memory didn't hold. Details slipped, sloppy and indistinct, like the edges of a bad photocopy. "Keep talking," I said, but nothing seemed to come out of my mouth. "Keep talking, Saf. Please."

"Christ, Aster. This is you." She wasn't there, couldn't be there, but somehow I heard her closer now. "You've got blood on your shirt."

I blinked, searching for some sign of her beyond the voice, but the magic held me in its grip. There was a crude Y of blood on my white shirt, stains left behind by the leaking sutures I'd pulled through too much activity. The pain rolled over me like a wave, then receded into an indistinct ache. "It hurts," I said, my voice low. "But I'll live."

Oscar Rasputin watched television in the lounge room. He hadn't even locked the door. Safia Mulani's voice followed me through the hallway, a faint whisper like a ghost on the fringe of my awareness. "Hey, Aster, what the hell..."

I lost the rest, diving into the memory. My world narrowed down to the barrel of the gun in my hand, the buzz of the television, and the short stretch of space between me and my prey. Something brushed my shoulder, tugged at me like an invisible hand, but I shrugged it off and stepped towards the door. A floorboard creaked, sagging under my weight. Oscar rose and turned, his eyes glistening with tears. "About time you made it," he said. "I've been waiting, Aster."

Part of me's surprised by that. I'd forgotten the tears.

The rest of me is twenty-eight again, still carried by the rage.

"Anya wants you dead," that part of me said.

"And I can't really blame her." Rasputin raised his hands, fingers spread. "Just do it, Aster. I know you've got to. We fucked up, we fucked up big time, and I'm sorry it was you."

"Shut up," I said.

"It's okay. I don't blame you." Rasputin's smile quirked, a familiar twitch. "Go on, pull the trigger. It'll be worse if you don't."

And then the moment before I shoot him there's nothing but details: a few styrofoam beans spilling out of the split in his beanbag; a convenience store hotdog on a napkin beside his bong; a new clip playing on the television, some best of the eighties countdown. Little things that register, then shatter with the sound of a gunshot. Oscar Rasputin, clutching at his stomach as he rolls away from the beanbag. "I'm sorry," he says, "We're all so sorry, Aster."

My second bullet caught him in the chest, right below the heart. It'll kill him, in time, but he'll need to bleed out. I pulled the needle nose pliers out of the waistband of my jeans and leaned over him, pulling his blood-slicked hand away from the stomach wound. It's enough, he's going to die eventually. There's enough faerie blood in him that an iron slug to the stomach will do that.

But someone who's me, but not quite me, says, "Hold still, Oscar. I'll need to remove some evidence in case my friends from the Force show up."

Queen Anya's Vengeance surges through me, thundering like a choir, telling me pain is necessary before the scales are even. There's a little part of me aware of Oscar slipping away, a fraction of his life force not quite there, but the best of him dies as I'm digging around inside him.

"Aster?" Safia's voice. Soft and frightened. And the spell shatters around me, the past giving way to the grubby realism of the present. I'm standing in an empty room with a gun in my hand, kneeling over a stain in the carpet. She's retreated, backing away from me, her eyes wide and her left hand reaching for the door. "Jesus, Aster. That was you."

I stood up, holstering the gun. "Yeah. That was me."

Safia's searching hand finally finds the doorknob and she halts her retreat, eyes moving from me to the stain on the floorboards. "He died?"

"Close enough. He had a back up plan, but Rasputin always did. It's why he picked the name."

"But you tortured him first."

"No. I tried to get at the evidence that'd link me to the killing."

Safia shook her head, cheeks slick with tears. "I saw your face, Aster. You enjoyed it, hearing him scream."

The room seemed too dark, too empty, too alien.

"That's torture, Aster." Safia stood in the doorway, ready to run. "I mean, fucking hell, there's nothing else you can call it."

"I called it a bad night," I said.

Safia shook her head. "I thought they were supposed to be the bastards."

"Yeah," I said. "I know."

After that I let loose with some tears of my own.

There was a cop car outside when we stumbled back into the daylight. One of those old white sedans that the Force liked to pretend were nondescript but tended to scream "cop" the moment you saw them. Kesey stood by the vehicle, umbrella held over his head and a grim look on his face. Goodman sat in the front seat, staying out of the rain. Kesey nodded and his partner fumbled with the door, trying to get out and cover the drive with his gun. I limped down the slope, exhausted rather than hurt, and Safia followed like the world's most reluctant shadow.

Kesey looked up at the house. "Didn't I tell you to stay away from murder scenes?"

"Wasn't aware I'd stumbled into any." I stamped on the little surge of anger and sorrow that tried to rise to the bait, forcing myself to breathe easy. "I'm here following up on Miss Mulani's case, Tim. How about you?"

"Waiting for you." He nodded to Goodman, then walked over to cover Safia with his umbrella. "We had an anonymous tip saying we'd find you here, along with another body. It seemed worth checking."

The rain plastered the few scraps of hair in Kesey's forelock against his skull, leaving the small bald spot bare to the elements. Exhaustion welled up in me, trickling out as a weary laugh. "Well, I'm here at least."

"No body?"

"Not yet."

The tension in Kesey's shoulders relaxed a little. "I hate when you say that," he said. "Just once I'd like to hear that there's no more bodies coming."

"When have either of us been that lucky," I said.

Kesey stared at me for a long time, trying to figure out the joke. I wasn't sure there was one, neither was he, so he settled for grunting and turning to Safia. "How about you? Anything to add?"

Safia's silence dragged on while the rain pattered against the long grass. Finally she came up with something, her voice tight and controlled. "Faeries."

"Isn't it always." Kesey rolled his eyes. "You know I'm going to have to detain the two of you, at least until I've given the house the once over."

"You're the boss," I said. "Just tell us where you want us to wait."

Kesey whistled Goodman over. The kid trudged through the rain, all smiles and teeth. "Hello, Killer. Fancy meeting you here."

"Just cuff 'em," Kesey said. "Get 'em out of the rain and hold 'em steady while I check things out."

"Sir." Goodman's voice dripped with mockery, ignoring the sorry figures we all made standing in the downpour. He made a point of pulling leather gloves from his belt before going for the cuffs, not even bothering to hide the fact that he might be fey-blooded. Kesey trudged up the hill, swearing as he slipped on the overgrown drive. We listened to the soft hiss of his grumbling monologue recede until Goodman closed the doors and trapped us both in the backseat. He hadn't frisked either of us, hadn't even taken Safia's knife. He returned to the passenger seat and rifled the doughnut box on the dashboard, pulling one free and saluting with it before he started eating.

"You're supposed to frisk us before you dump us in here," I said. "In case we're armed or something."

Goodman turned in his seat, his teeth sharp when he smiled. "Unnecessary. You're not going to cause trouble, Killer. Not here."

Safia pulled against her cuffs, testing them. "I might."

"Don't." Safia's head snapped sideways, her eyes cold and angry. "There was no tip calling him and Kesey out here," I said. "He wanted to talk to us, the two of us together. It's why he stabbed Colton and visited you afterwards."

Goodman beamed and brushed stray flecks of cinnamon off his drab tie. "Very smart, Killer. Very fucking smart. I knew I was going to like you."

Safia's eyes narrowed and she tensed for another kick. "You've got my sister?"

"No," Goodman said, "not yet, anyway. She's coming though, on the full moon. I just need Aster's help to open a gate."

"So, Goodman or Mordred," I said, hoping to cut him off. "Which one's the real name?"

"Neither, but you knew that, and I prefer Mordred to the other. You take what glory you can get when you're a half-breed bastard." He took another careful bite of his doughnut, but it wasn't enough to keep the oil from smudging the edge of his lip. "You know, I can understand why you liked this job, Aster. Doughnuts. Coffee. Lots of people fearing you, getting nervous when you're around. All those little urban myths that hover just below reality, all the names they call you. I think I could actually harness that and turn into a pig. Just for kicks. But it's doable. Very doable."

Safia pushed against the seat, the wet vinyl squeaking. I shook my head, trying to stop her doing anything stupid. "He's a faerie," I said. "They like to gloat."

"You wound me," Goodman said. "I don't know why more of us didn't think of this cop thing before, given the advantages. I mean, no-one looks at you, not really. They just see a badge and the little twinge of fear gets them in their stomach, like everything they've done wrong is laid bare because I looked at them. It's accurate, of course, in this instance, but I gather the mortals go on instinct more than anything else. It's quite delicious, that fear. I could get used to it, given time."

"You're wasting time," I said. "It won't take Kesey forever to realise there's no body here."

"True, but he's such a dear boy, he'll try to be thorough. He really doesn't want to find anything, Aster. In case you ever wondered. He's quite fond of you-"

Safia's foot hit the plastic partition, cracking against it with considerable force. I nudged her with an elbow, the only method of restraint available. Goodman grinned at us. "Temper, Miss Mulani. You really must control it. If nothing else, Aster will tell you, any well-equipped faerie sorcerer will use your anger against you if you give them half a chance. It's the reason Aster became such a grim, dour creature all those years ago. One of them, anyway."

Safia's voice hissed like a knife being drawn against a strop. "You took my sister."

"Not me," Goodman said, "others of my kind, yes. Older, more powerful, less tainted by mortal blood. I wish I could say who but I don't really know. It wasn't terribly important for the deal I struck with them."

I nudged Safia, cutting off her retort. "Yeah?" I said. "Which deal's that?"

"I want to go to Faerie," he said. "Same as every other half-breed with the misfortune of being begat on this side of the divide. They don't like us and they don't want us, so you've got to prove yourself before they'll let you through. Aster's friend, the pussy cat, he tried it the usual way. Work for the Queen, earn some favour, get yourself some dispensation. Seventy-odd years he did that, with no sign of a passport. I wasn't planning on waiting that long."

"That reminds me," I said, "what did you do with Oscar."

"I gave him to Gideon. Just like I said I would." Mordred laughed and rubbed at his eye, pulling a contact free on his fingertip. "The poor boy was rather disappointed, but I expect he'll recover in time."

"You're an arsehole," I said.

"And you're an annoyance," Mordred said. "Have you ever wondered why faeries are scared of you, Aster? Why they freak out at the very mention of your name? It's because you're the magical equivalent of unrefined plutonium. Twice dead, virgin-blooded, the true love of the Faerie Queen and who's still tethered to Her Majesty by unfulfilled Vengeance. There's so much potential there, so much power that it's almost obscene that it's only ever been used to bring you back to life."

"I don't think I'm going to fall for you, Mordred, so I doubt I'll do you much good."

"True, but there are other ways," he said. "The Leech is one and it's doing its part, but I still need blood. Your blood, Killer, and some of Miss Mulani's. The power to open a gate and a lodestone that'll find the missing twin."

"And now you've got us," I said. "So why not bring Uma back and be done with it?"

"Because it's not time yet," Mordred said. "Seeing you now is just a perk, a little professional courtesy." He folded his hands on the headrest, staring through the plastic. "I'm throwing a party, Aster. You'll know where and when it happens – all the magic I've leached out of your head won't give you any other choice. All I'm asking is that you come along willingly and let me harvest what I've planted. I'll get to go home, you'll be free of Her Majesty's Vengeance, and I can let poor Rick Duggan go back to his eternal peace and stop torturing him with little fragments of your memory."

"I don't party," I said. "Other people piss me off."

I caught a hint of sharp teeth beneath Mordred's smile. "You don't actually need to be there for this to work, Aster. I have

Dugan's skull, and the two of you are linked. He can come find you and get me all the blood I want. Having you there just makes things easier, promises less pain for all concerned, but make no mistake: I'll rip what I need straight out of you if that's what it takes."

"Rip away. I'm busy." I jerked my head towards Safia's side of the car. "Missing person's case."

"Yes, I can imagine. Tell you what – you agree to show up to my little shindig tomorrow and I'll return Miss Mulani's sister. The fey aren't going to return her voluntarily but I can force things Aster. I can make it happen. She returns to the land of the mortals, I get to go to the land of the fey. It seems a fair trade."

Safia turned to me, her eyes narrowed to slits. I shrugged. "Not that easy, otherwise you'd have done it."

"True, but it's a fair deal all the same." Mordred paused, sniffing the air. "Your old friend Kesey is coming back, Aster. Care to tell me your decision?"

"Get fucked." Safia winced when I said it, torn between the two possibilities and unsure of which she wanted. "I'm going to find you, Mordred, and you're going to regret it."

"Fair enough," he said. "I made the offer." His smile grew lopsided. "I wouldn't mention this conversation to Kesey, though. I've already hospitalised one of your friends, it'd be shame to injure another."

I glared at him, ready to burst, and he cut me off before I started in with the abuse. "Yeah," he said, "I'm an arsehole. But you also know I'll do it."

Kesey lumbered around the car and jerked open my door, breaking my stare when he dragged me out into the rain. "Nothing there," he said. "You and your friend should get going."

I turned and let him uncuff me. "You should watch out for your new partner, Tim. He's got some rough edges."

It earned me a crude little bark of laughter as Kesey glanced towards the car. He scowled. "Don't piss me off, Aster. Not now."

"We can go, then?" I glanced over at the car. Mordred grinned through the windshield, giving me a little wave. He said something to Safia I couldn't hear and she shrank back into the seat, a twist of fear running across her face. If Kesey noticed he said nothing, just produced the keys to the handcuffs and let me loose.

"Get out of here," he said, "and stay out of trouble, yeah?"

"Course." I stood there, watching Safia's face. "You know me, Tim."

"Yeah, I do. That's the fucking problem."

CHAPTER 10

Safia drove back to the city. I silently stared out the window, folding the anger up like a handkerchief and tucking it back in the pocket where I'd been keeping it for the last ten years. Most of it still fit. Most of it. Safia didn't say a damn thing, but I made her nervous now and that stuck in my side like a thorn. There was a line between duty and guilt and she'd watched me merrily cross it, gun in one hand and pliers in the other, Oscar Rasputin's blood slick against both.

"He wasn't exactly human," I said. "When you stop the fey, the really bad ones, it's just one of those things you need to do to keep the cops from figuring out the whole story. Iron slugs raise questions and sooner or later they'd figure it out."

Safia shook her head, eyes focused on the road. "Would it have made a difference?"

I thought about the answers to that, the little options that could make things better, the memories of Dugan's body back at the Palms. It wasn't me who pulled the trigger, not really. It wasn't me who stepped over the line, it was the magic goading me on. Pulling me across the boundaries of what I would and wouldn't do, then leaving me to rot once the deed was done.

Except it wasn't. There was still a little bit of me left in there, the bit that could have pulled back and said no. And I hadn't, not at first. I'd chosen not to, and afterwards I'd given in and said it wasn't my fault.

"No," I said. "Probably not."

"Then we shouldn't be talking about it." Safia adjusted the wipers, flipping them down a level and back again. After that she worked on the air-conditioning, trying to coax out a little more warmth. "Don't pretend, Aster, okay? Just, I don't know, get me back my sister."

The warm air made the cold worse, left the wet clothes clinging to me. "I can do that."

I closed my eyes, wishing I had a drink. I let the world recede and tried not to feel anything.

The ride back took longer than the ride out. The rain stopped halfway there, leaving us in a murky wet evening where everything gleamed. Safia didn't head home, didn't seem to be heading anywhere. We pulled into the parking lot of a McDonalds and Safia disappeared inside without a word. I didn't even notice until she reappeared with coffee, tapping her knuckle against the closed window. "Black, two sugars. If you squint real hard, maybe you can pretend it's real coffee."

The warm, burnt smell of cooking hamburger filtered through the car as I rolled down the window. "There's nothing in that cup that resembles real coffee."

She leaned against the car door, watching the car park. "You don't want it?"

"I didn't say that." It felt warm beneath my fingertips, little bright spots of comfort amid the cold. I pushed it into the palm of my right hand, the skin still tingling with the weight and kick of the phantom revolver. It felt good to overwrite the memory, to replace it with something immediate and tangible. Safia had her back to me. She made no move to get back in the car and I didn't try to get out. "Fuck, Saf. I'm sorry."

She straightened, her face pulled tight. "For what?"

I lowered my face, feeling the warmth steaming off the coffee. "Gimme the list. I'll start from the top and work my way down."

"Yeah. Well." She didn't finish the thought. "Just tell me you've got something useful out of that little escapade."

My smile pulled tight. "I got something. I need to kick seven kinds of shit through Gideon before I figure out what, exactly, but I'm okay with that."

It wasn't the right thing to say to someone who just watched you relive some of the worst moments of your life. Safia tensed up, and she pushed free of the car door that'd been holding her up. "You live in a very strange world, Aster."

"Not intentionally. It just happened."

"Bit by bit, right? Before you knew it?" She turned and looked at me through the window, smiling for the first time. "It's a strange world, and I'm not sure I like it here."

I took a long sip. It tasted terrible. "Me either. But it's what I've got."

"Yeah. I guess it is." She kneaded her shoulder. "Listen, I'm not going forward with you. Not after this. It's too much, Aster. There's no ... no centre to it, I guess. There's nothing to trust."

"I'll get your sister back."

"And I'll pay you for it," Safia said. "But I can't help anymore. You were right. I regret it. I'll drop you where you need to go and then, you know, I'm off. Just a client wanting the intel after the case is over. You were right, Miriam. I'm not a hero. I just take punches for them on TV."

"I get that. I'm okay with it." I tried the coffee again, pulled a face. "Hell, Safia, I'd prefer it like that, remember?"

"Good." She rounded the car, dumping her coffee into a garbage bin on the way and climbed back into the driver's seat. It took her two attempts to get the keys into the ignition, her left hand gripped the steering wheel so hard I thought she was planning on pulling it free. When the key finally slid in she just sat there, staring ahead. Our breath plumed in the cold air and the humidity left a smudge across the windshield. Safia took a deep breath. "Aster?"

"Yeah?"

"When you tell me the story, after you get Uma back?"

"Yeah."

"Lie to me," Safia said. "I don't think I want to know the truth about where she's been."

She looked ready to cry. In seven years, it was the first time she'd come close to tears.

"I can do that," I said. "The lying, at least, comes easy."

And I gave in to the anger, accepted it as inevitable. Dugan was wrong; it was nothing like the chaos of a wasps' nest disturbed, trying to swarm over me and send me in all directions. It was cold and full of clarity. It was like something clean I'd been resisting for far too long.

The shadow of the warehouses against the night sky looked like the black teeth of a cartoon skull, neat and evenly spaced, their only real menace their regularity. Safia dropped me on the corner, underneath the working streetlight, and I looked down the short road with its chain-link fences and the garage at the far end and the three dead cars in front of Gideon's hide-out. The streetlight at the far end of the block flickered a moment, trying to illuminate, but only lasted for a few quick flashes before giving up.

No-one answered when I knocked on the roll-a-door and the echo of it carried across the street, too loud for comfort. I edged around to the small door on the side of the building, the entrance to the little office with its deadbolt and lock. I held a flashlight in my teeth and fished the lockpicks out of my pocket, going to work while the cool wind gave me goosebumps. It took five minutes, longer than I wanted.

I eased my way in, leading with flashlight and gun. The interior office doorway was open, whatever door that'd been there, ripped off its hinges long ago. I shone the light through, found the small pile of rags and clothing that served as Gideon's bed. The car bodies lining the walls caught the light at weird angles. I could smell Gideon in there, his fear hung in the air like perfume. My flashlight caught something hidden in the empty wheel cavity of a dull green Holden, two bright eyes peering through the gloom. Oscar Rasputin's voice cut through the shadows. "Aster? Fuck, Aster, get outta here."

"Oscar?" I stepped through the doorway, gun first. That's as far as I got before the crowbar hit my wrist.

My grunt echoed across the small room while my revolver skittered to the floor. A second swing came in high, aiming for my head, and I dropped to the floor to avoid it, flashlight spinning a crazy pattern across the room as I held onto it in a death grip. The crowbar whistled through the air, making contact with the doorjamb with a solid thump. Gideon cursed beneath his breath, the weapon jarring against his hands, and I took the opportunity to scramble to my feet.

"I've got a gun, Aster," Gideon said. "The boss says it's messier, but we can make do with you dead."

I switched off the flashlight and edged back into the darkness, trying to keep quiet, but my wet sneakers squeaked on the dusty concrete. Gideon fired in my direction, the shot echoing. It went wide, ricocheted off a car body, but it stopped me in my tracks. I kept very still and listened to my heartbeat, the nervous skitter as Gideon moved along the walls, heading for the light switch. "I don't want to hurt you, Aster."

"Why don't I believe that, Gid? You could have answered when I knocked."

He flicked the switch and the overhead lights came on, the row of fluorescent tubes stuttering as they warmed up. Gideon stood by the larger doorway, gun pointed to my half of the building. My revolver sat between us, nestled against his pile of rags. "Don't," he said, the thin thread of anger in his voice cold and dangerous. "I may not be a great shot, Aster, but lead's cheaper than iron, and I've got plenty. I don't have to be picky about how many times I shoot."

"You fell in love with Rasputin, Gid. That kind of suggests you're not picky about anything."

I heard an angry snort from inside a dead car on the wall. I risked glancing over, spotted the red plastic cat-carrier half-hidden in the shadows. The light just caught the edge of Oscar's feline face as he pressed it against the steel mesh, ears pointed at the sky. "Play nice, Aster," he said. "One of us feels bad enough about things as it is."

"Shut up." Gideon edged towards my revolver, keeping me covered with his 9mm. "I wasn't going to do it, you know. Hand you over to Mordred, letting him open a gate."

I nursed my arm, watched his face, looking for some sign of control. "You just figured you'd set me up, twice, and see what happened?"

"No, not like that." Gideon glanced away, refusing to meet my eyes. "I figured I could stop him somehow, or cut a deal halfway through. I figured maybe I could just get Oscar back and we'd run for it before things got bad, before we had to kill someone."

"You can still do that, Gideon. I won't tell anyone you choked, and I'm sure Rasputin won't object to going home with you."

Gideon glared at me, the hesitation gone. "He's a cat, Aster. What the fuck am I supposed to do with that?" He fired another wide shot, tears forming in his eyes. "God fucking damn you, Aster. I loved him. It was enough to bring you back from the dead, it should—"

"You're not a faerie, Gid."

"I loved him so fucking much."

"Well, bully for you," I said. "He didn't love you back."

"Ah, Aster," Rasputin said. "Could we stop provoking my psychotic ex-lover?"

"Shut up, Oscar." I tried to move my arm and felt the pain ripple from my wrist to my shoulder. The anger worked against it, deadening the worst of it. "The fey use people, Gideon. They take and they take, and they don't give much back."

"Bullshit," Gideon said. "Oscar loved me, and you turned him into a fucking cat."

"You loved Oscar and he used you," I said. "It's been ten years, Gid. I've had him shacked up, safe as houses, with a friend of mine. He didn't exactly try and find you."

"Shut up."

"Come on, Gid. It's not like it's hard, once they're in your head. I've only got a fraction of their magic locked up inside me, all snug and second-hand, and I could have found you whenever I wanted."

"Shut up." Gideon sniffled, tears fogging up his glasses. The angry shred of magic caught in the depths of my heart unwound and flowed through me. I dropped forward, diving at my gun. Gideon's shot went wide, a second caught my leg. Mine nailed him, double-tap, right in the heart. A hard shot to make, left-handed and moving, but the magic made it easy. I barely felt the revolver kick. I sure as hell didn't feel the lead in my thigh. Gideon's body slumped to the floor. I took a few ragged breaths, bracing myself.

The Vengeance seeped out of me, leached away into the ether and left me nothing to buffer the pain. My body registered the full agony of my broken wrist hard enough to leave me gasping for breath, the wound in my leg dropping me to the floor a few seconds later. Outside the cold wind rattled against the roof.

It took a few minutes of screaming before I rode out the worst of it. I pushed myself off the concrete floor, knees creaking as I went. The bullet in my leg hurt like hell, but it was through-and-through, messy rather than deadly. I patched it with one of Gideon's old shirts, fumbling at the knot with my one good hand. It wasn't pretty but it stopped the bleeding and gave me some mobility, even if staggering over to the wrecked cars against the walls was enough to set me weeping. I leaned against the mangled metal, putting the weight on my uninjured leg. I waited for the cat to say something about killing Gideon. When he didn't I tapped the door to his cage. "You okay in there?"

"I'm in a cat cage," he said. "How 'bout you?"

"Had better days." I took a deep breathe and looked over at Gideon's corpse, tried to hold onto the anger that'd keep me from feeling bad about his death. "Poor, stupid bastard."

Oscar's face appeared at the side of the cage, looking at Gideon's corpse. "He really dead?"

"He's really dead."

"And Her Majesty's Vengeance?"

I shook my head, saying nothing.

"You stopped the Leech, though, right? Before you came to finish him off?"

I laughed. It wasn't a particularly pretty sound.

"Shit," Oscar said. "Just tell me Walt's alright and get me the fuck out of here."

"That much I can do," I said.

The cat's eyes peered out from the shadows of the old bomb. "I haven't really missed this, Aster. I just thought you should know that. I haven't fucking missed this shit at all."

I glanced back at the warehouse floor, at Gideon's blood pooling on the dusty concrete floor. "To be honest, Oscar, right now I don't really care what you missed. Just shut up and stay quiet."

I called a cab and waited, doing my best to clean up the mess and make myself look presentable. When the cabbie arrived he wasn't happy about the blood. He was even less pleased when I loaded the cat cage into the back seat with me. I gave him a fifty and the address of the local emergency room.

The cat whimpered the entire way. I hurt like hell but it didn't bother me. I passed out halfway there and stayed out 'til they were done patching up my injuries and loading me up with drugs to stave off the pain.

CHAPTER 11

Rick Dugan was waiting for me on the other side of consciousness. The same tree, the same sunset, the same shitty cigarettes. He flicked a butt in my direction, lit another behind a cupped hand. "Get up, Aster," he said, "we're not done yet, Danny and I."

I showed him the wreckage of my right wrist, the bruised and swollen skin visible even here. "I'm feeling pretty fucking done, Duggy. Gideon's dead. There's no more Vengeance to siphon off. Whatever the fuck you're up to, you can do it without me."

Dugan shook his head, scrawny strands of hair dangling down over his eyes. "Miriam, Miriam, Miriam," he said. "This was never about the Vengeance, not when you get right down to it." Skin sloughed away from his face. Feathers pushed through his pores.

I staggered to my feet, putting weight on my left leg. "Fuck off, Dugan. I'm tired."

There wasn't much left of his human face now, but the skull still managed to grin.

"Fine by me, sweetheart," the empty bone drawled. "I'm just passing through to repeat the boss's invite. He's got me on another job, collecting guests of honour."

"You can't rattle me by going after Safia, Rick. We already agreed that I don't love her."

"Sure we did, Aster," he said. "but you care about her all the same and you killed on her behalf. I mean, shit, who knows, maybe one of us was lying—"

I woke up in a hospital room, the green curtains pulled tightly around my bed. Kesey was sitting in the seat beside me, glasses perched on the crooked angle of his nose as he read the report in his lap. He didn't look at me, but he knew I'd woken up. "Nice thing about hospitals," he said. "They call the local precinct when murder suspects show up with bullet wounds. Do I want to know who put you in here?"

I pushed myself up with my good hand, struggling to a seated position. My throat was dry and the painkillers had wrapped the world in a soft layer I couldn't penetrate. On the other side of the curtain I could hear people walking around, doctors tending to patients and running between beds. "I'm missing a cat," I said. "Came in on the same cab I did, guessing they didn't bring him into the ER. I'm going to need him in a few hours. Think you could chase him up?"

Kesey's face went stony. He scratched at his right cheek with three fingers. "That kid they teamed me with," he said, "he does the same shit you used to do."

"Not quite the same shit, Tim." I shrugged and felt a sting of pain in my wrist beneath the blissful numbness of the painkillers. "I told you to watch him."

Kesey took a deep breath, patted down his pockets until he found a pack of cigarettes. He lit one for me, another for himself.

"Don't think we're supposed to smoke in here," I said.

"See if I care," Kesey said. "I'm here off the record, Aster. You know I hate doing that. Just tell me, okay?"

I shifted on the bed, retreating as best I could. We'd been here a hundred times, back when I was cop. Returned a few times afterwards when I started going freelance. Kesey never wanted the truth, not really. He wasn't built to handle the fey, the shades of grey and the casual bending of the rules. Kesey didn't want magic in his life.

"His name's Mordred, your sidekick," I said. "He's not entirely human and he'll gut you if he knows you know."

"Faerie?" Kesey spat the word, like he was afraid he'd choke on it.

"Not entirely," I said. "It'd be easier if he was. The kid has roots in the real world, that's probably how he faked his way into the Force. It's harder to run a fake ID through the system, harder still to fake the job when it burns every time you pick up a pistol."

Kesey mused on that for a moment, chewing his lower lip. "Goodman didn't show up for work today," he said. "No explanation so I paid a visit. His apartment's empty, hasn't been lived there for weeks."

"He's planning on taking a trip," I said. "I think that's why he was killing people, setting me up. He wants me good and pissed off when I finally go after him."

"Yeah? Why you, then, Aster. What makes you so special?"

"Because I'm a fucking idiot, Tim. I made the right mistakes all those years ago, and now I'm stuck paying for them over and over and over." I sank back into the thin mattress and sighed into the antiseptic air. "What the fuck are you doing here, Tim? Shouldn't you be chasing down leads or something?"

Kesey stood, brushing down his suit. "Safia Mulani's neighbours reported a disturbance four hours ago," he said. "The patrol found signs of a struggle and your client is missing. Unofficially for the moment, but let's be honest. Goodman's holding a grudge and he's had access to the cold case files for Dugan and that Russian you hung around with."

He pulled the curtain aside, hesitated before stepping out. "You know where he's going? Where and when?"

"I've got a fair idea."

Kesey nodded, not quite meeting my eyes. "They'll check you out in a few hours," he said. "They sent your cat to animal control. I'll have someone go get him in time for your departure."

I coughed into my arm to hide the laughter. "You don't approve of vigilante shit, Kesey."

"Who said anything about vigilante action," he said. "You've got a leg in a brace, Aster, and the bullet hole's fresh. There's no fucking way you're driving. We go, you stop Modred, I take care of the arrest in the aftermath. If anyone asks, Goodman fucked up on something mundane and no-one's any wiser."

"You could help," I said. "I sure as shit can't shoot straight with my good hand in a cast."

Kesey didn't bother giving me a reply for that one. I can't say I was really surprised.

We got there right on sunset, the rain plunging Marlowe Park into a dreary kind of twilight. It wasn't much to look at, just a long strip of greenery running between the river and the rows of old beach shacks on the far side of the road. Nothing to it at all, except someone'd left an old jacaranda tree standing when they landscaped the place a good fifty years ago and the combination of age and tangled roots were all they needed to establish a gate. Kesey had pulled up at the south end, a good twenty minutes limp from the tree. The revolver sat in my good hand as I stepped out of the car, the other arm strapped tight against my chest so it didn't hurt so bad. The waterfront was cold and wet and miserable, but at least the rain was thinning out.

I knelt and put down the gun, searching my pockets until I found a small knife I could use to cut the numb fingers on my right hand. The cat watched me, frowning, until I clicked my tongue at him. "Come here," I said. "I need your help and I don't have time to fuck around."

He backed away, fur sticking straight up. "Forget it."

"Virgin's blood for your help, Oscar. It's a straightforward deal."

"Not this time." The cat stared at me, its face serious. "We used to be good at this, Aster. We used to be a team. And since Mordred killed Gideon—"

"No," I said, wincing. "I did that."

"He pushed you to it," Oscar said. "Hell, we pushed you to it, ten years back when we lured you here. He had you kill Gid to get the Vengeance, he stabbed Walt to piss you off. He's fucking with my friends too, Aster. If you need help, I'll help. Save the blood to get your girlfriend's sister, if you still think that's going to be possible."

I hesitated. "Do you?"

Oscar lowered his head. "Not without killing someone."

I flipped open the barrel on the gun, making sure the remaining cold-iron slugs sat nestled in the nearest firing position. There were three left, not nearly enough to feel safe, but I had Colton's .32 tucked into my belt and that'd slow the bastards down if I really needed it done. "Mordred acquired Safia," I said. "I'm guessing he's got her here."

Oscar fell in beside me, just like old times. "A counterweight," he said. "If the gate's closed he needs something that'll call to the other side, something to keep it balanced while he tries to keep it open."

I listened to the steady scrape of my limp against the gravel path. "Just tell me how to stop it," I said. "You're my resident expert and I'm running low on options."

Oscar thought about that as we rounded the first curve and almost choked on the foul smell of a drain carrying sludge from the city drains to the river. "Two choices," he said. "Shoot him or compel him."

"They aren't good options," I said, my left hand jittery as I tried to hold the gun straight.

"They're what you've got." Oscar danced sideways, sidling into the shadows. "Keep 'em in mind, Aster. I'll do what I can." He disappeared and the memory of his first betrayal tugged at me, the moments before he set me up and let Dugan and Gideon shoot me. Part of me wished I'd compelled him, just in case, but the thought of sharing blood this close to Mordred and his pet made me a little nervous.

The path followed the river, wind rippling through the palms and dim lanterns lighting my way. It wasn't hard to spot Mordred as I rounded the second bend; the arsehole had the base of the jacaranda lit up with a trio of gas lanterns turned up bright. He was still two or three hundred metres away, barrel-chested and paunchy as he bent over the roots. I caught flashes of gold in his hand, a long feather being used as a quill as he laid the elements of his magic down.

It wasn't until I got closer that I noticed the Leech. It stood over the spread-eagled body of Safia Mulani, fascinated by the shallow cut they'd opened up in her stomach. They'd staked her down like a tent, the leather straps looped over her wrists and ankles were attached to heavy pegs, the Leech's solid weight pressing her shoulders down. Mordred scrambled over and sliced her belly with a knife, dipping the nib of his pen in her blood. "I know you're out there, Aster," he said. "I knew Gideon failed the same moment he died, and I knew you'd be coming the moment Kesey told you that your little friend was missing. You may as well come out, before I send Mister Dugan to find you."

There weren't enough shadows around him to sneak up and I didn't have the resources for subtlety. I walked forward with the gun held tight against my hip, subtlety be damned, keeping it steady despite the pain in my injured leg. "You'll be letting her go now, kid. Feel free to drop the pen, but if your hands do anything else I'll be happy to add a few holes where you're not really looking for them."

Mordred straightened, the bony ridge of his spine standing out against his bare back. "You've got that gun of yours, don't you Aster."

There wasn't much question in his voice and I didn't give him the benefit of an answer, just stepped into the light and let my eyes drift over to the Leech. The skull still smiled at me, unconcerned with the gun, but there were little points of light in the empty eyes now. A spark of life that focused on me, then flicked over to stare at its master.

"Gideon was supposed to bring me you and the cat," Mordred said. "He still would have died, but it'd make all this easier. Between you, your blood would have blown the gate open regardless of the edicts against it. The Lords of Faerie have power, Aster, but you two remain something else entirely. The faerie who cheated death and the twice-dead virgin. Even without the Queen's Vengeance upon you, you would have been enough. I can work with your hate, Killer. I can work with your attachment to this miserable little mortal. I can work with your fear."

"Sorry to disappoint," I said. "I don't want to speak for Oscar, but I'm kinda over being shit-scared of you and your little pet."

A strangled squeal emerged from the Leech, an ugly sound that rotated like water draining from a bathtub. I shuddered and the barrel of the revolver wavered, just for a moment. My shifting balance sent a spark of pain running down my leg, blood staining the torn hole in my pants as the stitches pulled open. I teetered, ready to fall, and the Leech squealed again.

"Harder, isn't it," Mordred said. "So many little injuries and so little of Anya's magic left to you."

My teeth ground together, fighting against the pain. "I only need to hit you once, arsehole."

"Go ahead." Mordred smirked and knelt among the roots, sketching a last symbol along the rough bark. "It doesn't matter if you shoot me, Aster. Not right now. Spill blood on these roots and the gate will open, and without me and the Leech to guide its destination it could open anywhere. There are worse things than me and my friend in Faerie, and you can bet they're itching to get another chance at the old stomping grounds."

I thumbed the hammer of the revolver. The Leech crouched down, feathered hackles rising. "This thing doesn't bleed," I said. "You'll have to try another one."

"It doesn't bleed." Oscar's voice came out of the darkness in the branches above, accompanied by the sound of claws against bark. "But I think it leaks, Aster. He's like a sponge, soaking up old emotions and channelling them here. Most of its anger is yours and Anya's. It'd be best to keep that contained."

"Your friend has a point there." Mordred looked up into the branches, squinting in the shadows. "I've started this. There's a gate opening here tonight and it'll need blood to control the destination. Hers will do, if you aren't willing to bleed, but the magic needs something to fuel it or things will go rather poorly for us and Miss Mulani's sister."

I limped forward, closing the distance. Mordred's face swam

in my field of vision, stretching as the pain pulled at the corners of my perception. I blinked, forcing myself to focus. "Neither of those options works for me."

Mordred finished his final rune and rose, holding his quill like a weapon. "They're the only ones you've got, Aster. Unless you know something about keeping a gate open, or picking its destination."

"Me, I know nothing," I said. "But it isn't like I'm alone, Danny."

"You mean you actually brought the cat?" He giggled to himself, wiping a hand across his bare belly. "That makes things easier."

Safia twisted, making use of the distraction, finding the strength to struggle against the restraints. I saw one give slightly, out of the corner of my eye.

"You really think you can stop me, Aster? No Vengeance, one hand, half your gun missing bullets."

"Fuck it," I said. "Yeah, I do."

The gun went off, impossibly loud in the open park. It bit a chunk out of the tree, the shot wide and useless. Mordred ducked anyway, grinning, his feet dancing a neat pattern between the roots of the tree as he backed away. He ended the movement crouched, arms wide and fingers splayed like claws, eyes glittering in the dim light. "She's yours," he said. "Bleed her."

The dark mass of the Leech surged forward, its horrid squeal approximating joy as it flew across the short stretch between us and bore me down. Sharp bone claws lashed out as I twisted beneath its weight, my body screaming in agony. The revolver went off again, kicking itself free of my loose grip. I didn't see where the bullet went. Didn't see where the gun went. Struggling against the Leech pulled my arm free of its sling, the pain hungry and sharp. I screamed. The Leech screamed. Something small and furry dropped out of the tree, a blur against the spotted canvas of my pain-wracked vision. Rasputin landed on the Leech's skull, claws scrambling against the exposed bone as the cat searched for purchase. The weight on my chest disappeared as the Leech clawed at its own face, trying to dislodge the feline.

I searched for the gun with my good hand, half-blind and weeping. My fingers found the barrel, pulling it close. I let my world shrink down to the solid, tangible presence of the dimpled rubber grip. Blood dripped down my hand, down my face.

The Leech pulled Rasputin off, throwing him at the tree trunk. The cat landed with a sick thump, bouncing away like a deflated ball before settling amid the roots. He twitched there, struggling to rise. The Leech turned back to me, the jaw of its skull clacking.

I pointed and fired, the heel of my good leg pushed against the dirt as I tried to scramble backwards. The shot hit the Leech's chest, a little off-centre. The dark mass shuddered, the mouth opening and keening at the sky. Energy leaked from the open wound, dark and shimmering like sunlight on an oil slick. The Leech sagged, staggering sideways. I fired again and the revolver clicked, the chamber empty. I blinked back tears, still pulling on the trigger, not quiet comprehending why the gun wasn't firing.

"You're out." Mordred loomed over me, kicking the gun in my hand. The sharp point of his quill hovered in my field of vision, the gleaming nib dangerously close to my eye. "No more moves now, Killer. Time to bleed."

"Fuck off," I said, spitting the words at him.

"No," he said. "It's time, Aster. I'm going home."

The gunshot came from behind my head, a distinctive soft crack that's never quite as loud as the movies make you think it should be. Blood fountained out of Mordred's arm, running around his elbow. The second shot caught him in the chest, sending him staggering backwards. Kesey's voice came out of the darkness, hovering around the fringes of my vision. "On the ground, arsehole, or the next one's going through your fucking skull."

Mordred pressed a finger against the wound in his chest, watching silvery blood bubble around it. "Lead," he said, giggling. He breathed in and the pain flashed across his face, but I knew it wouldn't last. Kesey fired again, bullet glancing against Mordred's skull. The half-fey laughed even louder, silver blood seeping from the gash against his face. He took a staggering step sideways, closer to the tree roots. Kesey moved forward, crouching over me, the gun still trained on Mordred. "Keep shooting," I said, forcing the words out. "Keep fucking shooting."

Kesey followed orders, emptying the clip. Mordred gave ground, smirking all the way, waiting for the stillness that followed. His retreat took him closer to the Leech, right next to the big mass of the beast as it slumped beneath the tree branch.

"You can't kill me with lead," Mordred crowed. "Fucking hell, Aster, I thought you knew better than this." Then he screamed as one of the tent-pegs holding Safia down punched into his leg, right below the knee.

Safia twisted the short length of metal, a second peg dangling loose from her other wrist. She pulled the cheap steel free and stabbed again, blood flicking off the bent point as she swung.

A few silver drops fell onto the bloody writing on the tree roots, going as dark and crimson as any human's as the symbols sucked the magic out of it. The Leech froze and exhaled, its stored magic leaking from it like shimmering threads of light. Mordred stared at the spilt blood for a moment, then he started howling.

"Blood's blood," I said. "And you're a fucking arsehole."

The energy shivered through the air, just like a compulsion. The Leech went first, deflating like a balloon, and I felt the sharp tug of the magic latched from my soul as the creature's form sank against the roots. Mordred watched it go, eyes wide, his narrow face pale in the gas light. Then he wheezed out a hollow breath and fell forward himself, his body a lifeless husk draped over a bump in the tangled roots.

Silence descended. Somewhere in the hollows of the tree's root system, a knot of rainbow lights boiled in a rapid pattern.

Kesey reloaded his gun, the new clip sliding in with a soft click. "Fucking hell, Aster, what the fuck is that?"

"Something you didn't see when you write your incident report." I tried to push myself upright and failed. "Shut up and help me, Tim."

Kesey's hands pulled me upright, half-carried me over to

Safia. The gate to Faerie pulsed, growing a little larger. The seams in the knotted rainbow gave me glimpses of another world, little slices of Faerie flowing past as the real world tried to unravel the light. I knelt and tugged at the stakes holding Safia's ankles to the ground.

"That's..." The words faltered, her voice unsteady, and she sagged against me, one hand pressed against her stomach wound as if she'd be able to keep the blood from flowing. I pushed her back, getting her away from the tangle of lights and the inscription.

"Yeah," I said, "that's the way to Faerie."

"Shit." Kesey's eyes grew a little wild. "What happens next?"

"It gets bigger," I said. "And when it's done, when it's open, something comes through. And if it's the wrong thing, well, then we're all pretty much fucked."

We stood there for a moment, two of us broken and bleeding. The sounds of Faerie flowed through the gate, a faint laughter like tiny bells playing in the air. I turned to Kesey. "Go see if the cat's alive," I said. "If he's not, then it's probably a good time to run."

CHAPTER 12

It should have been pretty, but it wasn't. The air stank of pine needles and the harsh perfume you get from flower-scented car deodorizers, a sharp permeation of the scents I'd been expecting when the little knot of rainbow light unravelled and opened out. Faerie sat there, on the other side of the light, like a postcard viewed through layers of coloured frost. It should have been pretty, the home of Goddamn faerie tales and all, but it wasn't. The entire place was filled with assholes and it'd gotten worse with time, shut away from the real world and desperate for mortals to torture.

Safia put a hand on my shoulder, leaning on me for support. Her eyes didn't leave the knot. "My sister's in there?"

"In there." I took a deep breath, steadying myself. Part of me worried I'd fall with her weight there, light though it was. I felt like a scrap of cloth, ready to get lost on the wind whistling through the rift, a soft exhalation of another world trying to convince ours to deliver mouth-to-mouth. "It'll be short-lived, but we can use it."

Safia took a step closer, leaving her hand on my shoulder as a tether. "We can get her out?"

"Maybe. Maybe not. Only one way to be sure."

"I took her hand off my shoulder and held it, rubbing a thumb across her palm. Rasputin sat nestled in Kesey's arms, heedless of the terrified expression on the old cop's face. One of the cat's legs hung at a bad angle, and there were tufts of fur missing from his raised hackles. "It's magic. It's just magic. Danny opened it, asked it to bring him what he needed. We can work with that, maybe, if you want it to work, but something needs to go through before the damn thing collapses."

"It's another world, Aster." Safia's voice rose, getting wobbly around the edges. "A whole 'nother fucking world." She tugged her arm, trying to break free of my grip, but I held on.

I looked down at the cat. "Just like the old days?"

"Right down to almost getting us both killed."

I stood on wobbly legs, regarding the bright bloom of the gate. "What do I do?"

"Compel it, same as everything else," Oscar said. "Then lie back and think of England. It should do the rest."

"At least the blood should be easy to get." I raised a bloodied palm, the hair on my arm tingling as I pushed it towards the gates. I grit my teeth and rested the broken hand on Safia's shoulder. "Think of Uma," I said. "Think of how badly you want her back."

Safia opened her mouth to say something, but I never heard it. Her hand wrapped around the mangled mess of my right wrist, a soft tingle of pleasure beneath the pain and panic of what I had planned. My good hand reached out towards the light, pushing into the knot of colour at the edge, letting the writhing hues start braiding their way across my fingers.

It hurt, worse than before. I was okay with hurt. I'd hurt plenty of people, been hurt plenty myself. A small part of me registered the pain and closed it off, sealing it away as best I could. Another part of me registered the sound of Safia screaming, trying to pull free of my grip, trying to get away from the slow tangle of colour creeping up my forearm. It hurt her too, even using me as a buffer. I stayed tethered, refusing to let go, ignoring the panic. Magic's exhausting and it causes pain, but it's only in the mind.

"Uma," I said. Or maybe I didn't. Everything sounded far away, lost amid the roiling white noise like you get when you press a shell to your ear. My fingers dipped into the lands of Faerie, getting nipped by the stark winter cold. I felt something bite my thumb, drawing blood. Fey were like that, some of them, fast and vicious, but it wasn't real until I got sucked through. I wouldn't be dead until I gave all the way in and followed the weave, letting the tangled threads of light transport me from the real world to another.

I thought of Safia, tried to keep her fixed in my mind. Harder than it sounded, given the circumstances. Never thought it'd be a problem, myself. The litany was simple: I didn't let go until it gave me what I wanted.

Time shattered and ceased to have meaning, just like Einstein always said it would. One minute of ecstasy goes too fast, and a minute of pain like this unfolds into a lifetime.

I held fast, refusing to let go, forcing my aching fingers to grab at something on the far side.

Then the rift gave me what I was looking for, a cold hand wrapping around mine. I held onto it and pulled, trying to rip my way free of the tangle of light.

Uma Mulani came with me. I don't remember much after that, not for a while.

When I came to, Safia was comforting her sister, holding her tight while Uma lay in a whimpering heap on the ground. Safia cooed softly, her voice soothing in the night. In the distance I heard sirens.

Rasputin nudged his nose against my thigh. "You do believe in faeries."

I called him an arsehole and passed out again. It seemed like the thing to do at the time.

The cops showed late. They always did, when the fey shit is involved. I'd helped Rasputin and Anya Titan set up those habits years ago. Little nudges and twists in what people thought would happen and it became ingrained, a self-fulfilling loop. That's how it always is, with faeries. I sat in the back of an ambulance, using the door to keep me upright. Kesey took care of things, telling the right lies. He didn't look at me the entire time, didn't say a damn thing.

On my own again, I guess. I could live with that.

Oscar sat in my lap and nuzzled against my chest. I flicked him behind the ear. "None of that."

"I'm a cat, Aster. It's how we scent things."

"You're an arsehole, arsehole, and if you try it again I'll hand you to the pound as a stray."

Oscar snorted and rested his head against my knee. I scratched him behind the ear and he purred, needling my uninjured thigh with his claws. It was pleasant enough, but I'd never be a cat person. "Don't get used to this," I said.

"I wouldn't dare."

"And you're not living with me."

Oscar's purr rolled like a soft chuckle. "Aster, I've seen your apartment. You couldn't pay me to live there."

Then we sat there in silence for a while, watching the cops do their thing as they secured the crime scene and let the ambulance boys do their thing with the injured. Safia and Uma had a spot to themselves, both of them getting checked out by an EMT. Safia talked constantly; her sister huddled under the silvery thermal blanket they'd given her and watched the world through wide eyes. Experience said they'd write her state off as shock, maybe even a touch of craziness as a result of the trauma, but if Safia kept her head it'd go down okay. She'd settled on a story before the cops arrived, something about Mordred holding Uma hostage and trying to get a ransom, and I'd improvise if the cops started asking me questions. I wasn't expecting much. Kesey would cover for me, even if he'd hate himself afterwards.

They lifted a dead body onto a gurney and carted what was left of Danny Mordred away to the morgue.

My arm spent six weeks in a cast. I didn't take any calls, didn't answer the door, didn't even leave the house until the damn thing came off. After it did, I headed down to Walt's bar and drank a cup of coffee, watching the suits head in and out. The kid behind the bar said Walt wasn't back yet, that he'd taken a few weeks leave after getting out of hospital. I nodded and thanked him and ordered another coffee, wondering why it didn't help to hear the old bastard was okay. The second coffee went down bitter. I was just thinking about leaving when the kid delivered a gin, the booze clear and cold in its glass. "From the lady by the counter," he said, pointing. Safia waved, her expression neutral. I nodded, calling her over.

"You're a hard woman to find," she said. "I phoned a few times."

"I've been on sabbatical." I drained the last of my coffee before moving on to the alcohol. Safia sat there, watching me, her eyes brown and gleaming in the bar light.

"I took in the cat," Safia said. "I know it's probably a bad idea, but I figured I owed him after he helped me."

"Your choice, just don't let him watch you in the shower," I said, "and tell him to watch where he's putting his paws. He may look cute, but he spent two hundred years as a letch and an arsehole and I've never met a faerie who didn't go both ways when it suited them. He'll use the cat excuse every chance he gets but he doesn't think like one."

"He's been good."

"Yeah?" I tapped the edge of the gin glass, looking for ways to keep my hands busy. "He must like you, then. Just keep him away from company, otherwise the conversations get messy."

"So, I've got your cheque," Safia said. "Seven years later than I expected, but you did the job."

"Yep." I didn't ask about her sister. Safia didn't offer. Most of the details were public already, courtesy of the tabloid articles about Uma Mulani's mobster ordeal. She was spending some time collecting herself, away from the press, but there were already rumours of a triumphant return to acting once the doctors declared her sufficiently recovered. The waitress stopped by, delivering a Coke to Safia.

"Here." Safia slid an envelope in front of me. "And done."

I concentrated on the drink, refusing to look down. "Thanks."

"Fuck, Aster." Safia toyed with her drink, turning the glass with her fingertips. "I owed you money for the job. I paid it. You're not meant to make a girl feel bad for that."

"Same rules as always, Saf." I turned to look her in the eyes. "You're a client. Feelings don't come into it."

"The case got closed, Aster. You've been paid. That's not going to work anymore."

The hope in her smile was like a knife to my stomach. "It's got to," I said. "The other options, whatever you're thinking, they aren't options. It'll hurt less if you let it go."

"Yeah?" She put a hand on my forearm, halting my attempt to take another drink. "And what if I refuse to accept that?"

I tried to pull free, but she held firm. A tiny drool of gin spilled over the side of my trembling glass and dribbled down to my finger. "I can't do it, Safia," I said. "I'm broken. I've been broken for a long time. You don't get other people caught up in that, not if you've got a choice. Not if, you know, there's..." I searched for the word and came up with nothing. "Yeah, well, you just don't."

"I get it." Safia let go of my arm and folded her hands in her lap. "I mean, I saw you in the house Aster. I saw what happened. I get what you're running from, I really do, and Oscar filled me in on the rest. I know why. I know about the scars."

"I showed you those, remember?"

"I wasn't talking about the ones on your chest," Safia said. "Those faeries fucked you up, didn't they?"

"Maybe." I drank fast, without even tasting the gin. "You get it, though, right?"

"Yeah, I do." Safia leaned forward and kissed me on the cheek, her lips soft. "I get it. And I think you're wrong."

She stood up, pulling her coat over one arm. "The cat said I should tell you two things before I left, just in case it made a difference."

"It won't."

"Humour me." She put a hand on my shoulder, left it there until I turned and looked her in the eyes. "First up, he told me to remind you that he's not actually dead and Gideon was self-defence."

"Fucking Rasputin." I snorted and gave her a sad, weary smile. "I know that."

"Good." Safia's eyes pinned me, held me in place before I could use the momentary relief from seriousness as an escape. "He also said I should remind you that you're not actually a faerie." She leaned forward and tapped my chest, right above my heart. "You're one hundred percent human, Aster. Just because you need something, it doesn't mean you're using people. Sometimes you're allowed to be happy. And sometimes the people who like you don't actually want a damn thing."

"They always want something," I said, my voice low. I'm still not entirely sure who I was trying to convince.

"Your call," Safia said. "I just thought you should know."

And she kissed me again, gently, and I didn't have it in me to stop her. She tasted of sugar and caramel. A promise of the future I kept telling myself I didn't need.

When I opened my eyes Safia was smiling, a little too pleased with herself. "I'll see you around, Aster."

Then she turned and walked away. I watched her go, lips tingling, waiting to see if she turned back.

AUTHORS NOTE

I DIDN'T MEAN TO WRITE THIS...

AN AFTERWORD

The two novellas in this collection were never meant to be published. I write the first draft of Horn at Clarion South in 2007, typing away in the sweltering Queensland heat.

We'd been warned the upcoming tutor hated stories of the "unicorn and fourteen-year-old girl" genre of fantasy, and I took it as a personal challenge. I figured the story would be read by the eighteen people in the workshop room, giving me a chance to prove some vague point, then I'd file it away in the folder of unfinished drafts.

That early draft of Horn is rougher and considerably shorter, but many of the core elements are already in place. Aster's burnt out, called in on a job, and ends up dead halfway through the story.

It was rough and crude and pressed people's buttons, but the damn story stuck with people, and took on some notoriety. Successive instructors read it and gave me notes. People outside the workshop asked questions about it, and urged me to finish the story. What started as a short story became a novella, and even then I largely wrote it to get certain people to stop asking about it.

It is, after all, a novella that features unicorn pornography going terribly wrong. It's a pulp novel featuring queer protagonist, written by a predominately white, CIS-presenting, and largely straight chap. For all that I've tried to approach the character with respect and awareness of just how prone white, straight dudes are to fucking up when writing such things, the knowledge that I would fuck up loomed large.

That Aster found her way to a larger audience owes a huge debt to Angela Slatter. She read early drafts and offered great comments, then suggested she might pass it on to Perth's Twelfth Planet Press,with a personal recommendation. Something akin to, "you're going to hate this story, but you'll also want to publish it."

It proved to be prophetic.

Twelfth Planet put out the first edition in 2008 and it was—by the standards of Australian short fiction—a smash hit. They put in the request for a second book, and would have gladly done a third if health issues hadn't derailed my writing for the better part of six years.

And yet, Aster holds fast in people's memories. Horn's seen the occasional reprint here and there, and over a decade after Bleed came out, people ask about the third Aster novella.

I'm not sure I could actually write Aster today. *Horn* was written by a younger, angrier, lonelier Peter who broke up with his fiancé (as so many people do) in the aftermath of Clarion. The Peter of 2023 is generally fatter, happier, and pleasantly married to a rather smashing spouse. To say nothing of the conversations about own voices, representation, and intersectional issues have grown increasingly nuanced and widespread in the last fifteen years.

For all that, Aster is one of my favourite characters I've written, and for all their faults these books bring glee to my pulp fiction loving heart. I hope to write another Aster book one day, and hope you may be around to enjoy them too.

But I will admit, I understand entirely every time someone taps out and declares this isn't their jam as a reader.

—Peter M. Ball
March 31, 2023
Brisbane, Australia

ABOUT THE AUTHOR

PETER M. BALL is an author, publisher, and RPG gamer whose love of speculative fiction emerged after exposure to *The Hobbit*, *Star Wars*, David Lynch's *Dune*, and far too many games of *Dungeons and Dragons* before the age of 7. He's spent the bulk of his life working as a creative writing tutor, with brief stints as a performance poet, gaming convention organiser, online content developer,

non-profit arts manager, GenreCon convenor, and d20 RPG publisher.

He's the author of the Miriam Aster series and the Keith Murphy Urban Fantasy Thrillers, three short story collections, and more stories, articles, poems, and RPG material than he'd care to count.

He's the brain-in-charge at Brain Jar Press, an aspiring made scientist running publishing experiments through Eclectic Projects, and resides in Brisbane, Australia, with his partner and a very affectionate cat.

Find Peter Online at PeterMBall.com or reach out to Peter on your favourite Social Media platforms:

facebook.com/PeterMBall

twitter.com/PeterMBall

instagram.com/PeterMBall

goodreads.com/PeterMBall

patreon.com/PeterMBall

ALSO BY PETER M. BALL

SHORT STORY COLLECTIONS

The Birdcage Heart & Other Strange Tales

Not Quite The End Of the World Just Yet: Short Stories & Strange Futures

These Strange & Magic Things: Short Stories

MIRIAM ASTER NOVELLAS

Horn

Bleed

BRAIN JAR PRESS SHORT FICTION LAB

The Early Experiments

Winged, With Sharp Teeth

8 Minutes Of Usable Daylight

A White Cross Beside A Lonely Road

One Last First Date Before The End Of The World

Shedding Skins

ESSAYS

You Don't Want To Be Published & Other Things Nobody Tells You When You First Start Writing

THANK YOU FOR BUYING THIS ECLECTIC PROJECTS CHAPBOOK

To receive special offers, bonus content, and info on new releases and other great reads, sign up for our newsletters.

To get more from the author, Peter M. Ball, you can sign up for his newsletter at PeterMBall.com